TIN TOYS

Ursula Holden was born in Dorset, one of five children. She lived in Egypt as a child and went to school in the south of England, where she was frequently accused of 'dreaming'. She was in the WRNS during the War, then moved to Dublin for several years. She has worked at a number of jobs – waitress, hat-check girl, artists' model, library assistant, saleswoman, and cleaner. She has three daughters and lives at present in West London. She did not begin writing until her early forties, but has written to date nine novels, *Endless Race* (1975), *String Horses* (1976), *Turnstiles* (1977), *The Cloud Catchers* (1979), *Penny Links* (1981), *Sing About It* (1982), *Wider Pools* (1983), *Eric's Choice* (1984) and *Tin Toys* (1986), as well as some short stories.

TIN TOYS

URSULA HOLDEN

A Methuen Paperback

A Methuen Paperback

British Library Cataloguing in Publication Data

Holden, Ursula
  Tin toys
  I. Title
  823'.914[F]   PR6058.0434

  ISBN 0–413–15850–0

First published in Great Britain 1986 by
Methuen London Ltd
This edition published 1987 by
Methuen London Ltd
11 New Fetter Lane, London EC4P 4EE
Copyright © Ursula Holden, 1986

Printed and bound in Great Britain
by Redwood Burn Ltd, Trowbridge, Wiltshire

The extract from W. B. Yeats' 'The Circus Animal's
Desertion', *Collected Poems*, is reprinted with kind
permission of Michael B. Yeats and Macmillan London Ltd.

Now that my ladder's gone,
I must lie down where all the ladders start,
In the foul rag-and-bone shop of the heart.
W. B. Yeats

I would like to thank the Corporation of Yaddo, Saratoga Springs, New York and The Tyrone Guthrie Centre at Annaghmakerrig, Monaghan, Ireland, for inviting me to stay while I was working on this book.

ONE

I could be certain of happiness on Saturday mornings because of my dancing class. Each week I went there with my nurse to join the rest, all escorted by nurses or maids. Servants were usual then, in the days before the War, though I felt different even then. The other little girls seemed fond of their nurses and I hated mine. She wasn't a proper nurse but an elderly aunt, who years ago had looked after my father when he was young. Papa was dead now. She had come to look after me and my baby brother and she had to be called Nurse, not Aunt. Mamma said she could consider herself lucky, under the circumstances, to work for the family again. Nurse seemed a suitably cold and unfriendly name for a cold unfriendly person, whose only interest was in Bruno, the newborn boy in the shawl. She didn't like me. Little girls were a nuisance, they fussed insistently, they asked too many questions, they stared, worst of all they were sneaky in their ways. She ignored me as far as possible but on Saturdays she left Bruno and took me to Miss Dance's class. I wore my cream Viyella frock to skip and curtsey to Miss Dance's simple tunes and I forgot about Bruno. I would rather have gone with Maggie our housekeeper, but Mamma preferred Nurse to take me.

The year that Bruno was born was when I first saw Lucy, just before Christmas, at Miss Dance's Saturday class. There was a Christmas tree like a silver spire by the doorway. Each pupil was allowed to place her doll or teddy bear under the lower branches before the dancing began. Our skipping and curtseying was observed by the button-eyed dolls peering from their silvery bower. My toy was different, it was a giraffe made of tin, old and dented. I was the youngest there. I hopped to Miss Dance's playing and forgot that I had two elder sisters and an awful brother wrapped in a shawl.

'Dance your feelings my little dears. Make it a dance of love,' called Miss Dance.

I was nearly seven. Already I knew that feelings were better kept to yourself. I stamped and jumped and grinned. I liked the grand march past best, finishing with a curtsey to Miss Dance which she called '*la grande révérence*'. She received our homage by the side of her silvery tree, wearing a long skirt and a silvery lace blouse. After curtseying we retrieved our toys and went home. We liked her and I'm sure she liked us. For that hour we belonged to her, twelve little girls and their dolls. To us she seemed a bright being revealing another world from her upright piano or standing beside her tree.

Children's nurses, governesses and nurserymaids were a part of life in those days. Compared with the rest of the children at the dancing class our house was understaffed. Nurse, in reality an aunt, ruled the nursery for Bruno and me. My two sisters, Bonnie and Tor took lessons from an old governess who lived outside our town, coming to the house every day. The cooking and cleaning was done by Maggie from Ireland. Apart from Bruno it was a house of women. My mother was rarely at home and when she was we hardly saw her. Apart from Saturdays I didn't mix with other children. Bonnie and Tor were due to start school after Christmas when Gov would retire for good. My sisters loved Gov. The schoolroom was their private world.

The nurses waited outside while we danced. They talked and held copies of *The Lady* and *The Nursery World*. Miss Dance liked to have us alone, so that our loyalties wouldn't stray. The nurses didn't read the magazines, preferring to rival each other as to the affluence and social status of the families they ruled. If a mother turned up she was made to feel inferior, having trespassed outside her domain.

Miss Dance singled me out with special smiles, because I had no father now. I was a pale child, and particularly quiet since my brother was born. I didn't know that I was pretty, having been made to feel self-conscious about a patch of white in my hair. My sisters had normal hair but all three of us had rather dingy teeth. Nurse said that this came from early neglect, but our teeth were strong in spite of their colour. Bruno, who was all she cared about, was still toothless, hairless and red.

'Very good, Ula. Keep trying. Wave your arms. Smile.'

Sometimes I practised at home when Nurse wasn't looking, pointing my toes and waving. I loved being praised by Miss Dance. I loved putting my giraffe under the tree with the dolls. I disliked dolls. That day there was a black stuffed monkey there.

'Lovely, Ula, Now for the grand march past. Take your partners, now then.'

I didn't look round. I preferred to march alone.

'Ula, you take Lucy.'

'I don't know her.'

'Don't be unfriendly, dear. The march is done in pairs and Lucy is our guest.'

She wanted to make Lucy feel wanted. Lucy's aunt was a friend of Miss Dance and Lucy was on holiday here. Lucy had dark curls and brilliant eyes, the colour of Wedgwood china. She was the tallest child in the class that Saturday and she had a haughty air, moving swiftly on arched feet that turned outwards. Her ankles looked delicate under her skirt of bright pink pleats. Her dark hair smelled of lavender water, her hand was cool in mine.

'Good, Ula and Lucy, point those toes. Good.'

Lucy made me feel clumsy and sticky-handed. I was afraid I'd leave a mark on her dress. It was a lovely bright shade of pink, with piped seams and short enough to show her knickers when she moved. My own cream Viyella seemed dowdy, I felt ashamed again of my hair. I clutched her hand, I kept my lips closed over my dull teeth. You had to pause when you came to the tree where Miss Dance stood, you held your skirt out, bending low over your extended right foot. I looked up. My giraffe, which I called Tin, had fallen, his legs stuck stiffly up. The black monkey, dressed stylishly in a ballet skirt, belonged to Lucy. The class was over. Time to pick up our toys and leave. Lucy elbowed me aside rudely, she pulled a tremendous face at me. We hadn't spoken to each other but I thought she was spellbinding. I had never seen anyone touch their nose with their tongue. I kept my lips closed in a line as we went down the passage to where the nurses were.

I knew Nurse wouldn't like Lucy. She didn't like me to make friends. Anyone other than Bruno was an intrusion on her time. I could think of no greater joy than holding Lucy's hand. Nurse hurried me into my coat. 'Oh hurry, Ula.' She was worried about Bruno's lunchtime bottle. I had something of Lucy's in my palm. If you kept something belonging to a person you might see them again, you might have luck as well. I clenched the wisp of pink silk from her dress and thought about her. Her dancing shoes were red instead of black or bronze, her hair was ringleted, her lavender scent and her eyes were wonderful. Nurse was rough-handed, pulling my hair from my coat collar, jamming my beret on, begrudging me her time. She had seen Lucy pulling a face. Ill-bred child, she had no place here. What a shocking shade of pink. And such curls, were they permanently waved? The girl had showed her knickers, as well as having no nurse, or even a mother. Her father had brought her, there he was waiting outside. A blessing they didn't live here and wouldn't be staying long. Not our kind, oh no. They were Irish as far as she knew.

I watched Lucy take her father's hand. She wore a dark green coat and nothing to cover her curls, more dashing than the berets I and my sisters wore in the winter. Her father wore brown tweed. Nurse pushed me ahead of her. The other nurses didn't know she was really an aunt; that knowledge would have set her apart, they would have ostracized and distrusted her. The rest met at the parties given for the children to which I and my sisters were never asked. To be asked you had to give parties back; our family kept to themselves. I didn't miss the parties, not knowing what they were like. Dressing in my cream Viyella frock was my weekly treat in spite of Nurse's resentment. She hated leaving Bruno with Maggie, who though good-hearted was untrained to English ways. I loved Maggie. 'Oh hurry, do, Ula. Why don't you smile?'

I tried to put my giraffe under my coat as I ran to keep up with Nurse along the main street of our town. She told me to have respect for my clothing and to keep my toes pointed straight, I wasn't at the class now. Nurse didn't care what I thought or how I passed my time as long as I was quiet and kept clean. I looked back at Miss Dance's window and the glittering boughs of her tree. Nurse thought that silver trees were cheap-looking, on a level with Maggie's taste.

'Will Mamma be coming home soon? Will we have a Christmas tree?' She said that my mother didn't confide in her, that Gov was her confidante. Nurse had a hoarse voice, unlike Maggie's, and angry-looking eyes.

Mamma had not been home for six weeks. Bruno was over two months old. Mamma preferred London and her theatrical friends to being with us in the country. Nurse thought her flighty and bad. I think she even blamed her for Papa's death from a heart attack. A reason for her loving

13

Bruno was that he looked like Papa had as a baby. Nurse was an aunt by marriage, with dark skin round her eyes and hair like crinkled white wire. She had very black eyes that looked darker when she was vexed. Her yellow fingers had mauve-nailed tips. She never mentioned her own family, but only my father as a child. I had no pity for her. I had heard Mamma talking with contempt about homeless people or those of mixed blood who never fitted in. She had done Nurse a favour, employing her; other people's children were Nurse's concern, she was expected to love Bruno as once she had loved my Papa.

'Mamma wants to act, doesn't she?'

'She doesn't confide in me, I've told you. Who am I to know what she wants? Gov knows it all, I dare say.'

Both she and Maggie resented Gov who had Mamma's entire trust. Years ago Gov had taught Mamma her lessons, but Gov was differently placed from Nurse. She paid the bills for Mamma, running our house smoothly, but going home to her own cottage at night, in Shottermill. It was Gov who had employed Maggie, Gov who ordered the groceries and bought our clothes. She would do no household chores, she returned each night to her cottage and her privacy, arriving each morning at nine. She lived apart in the schoolroom with my sisters. At night Maggie saw them to bed, and looked after them at weekends, and Bruno too while Nurse took me to Miss Dance. Bonnie and Tor were secretive, they didn't require Maggie's care. They stayed downstairs in the schoolroom with the door shut, they never let me inside. I longed to find out what they did in there, and what they learned with Gov.

Resentment over Gov gave Nurse and Maggie a bond of a sort. Gov gave herself too many airs.

As we reached our gateway I could hear my sisters talking. The schoolroom window was wide, though it was a cold day. They sounded excited, it was rare to hear them laugh or make any sound. I ran over.

'Look, Nurse. They've put up a tree.'

Nurse didn't look into the window. I went inside ahead.

Gov practised thrift and frugality, she made all my sisters' clothes: serviceable grey or navy skirts, hand-knitted jerseys to match. In winter we wore hand-sewn cotton pants under our bloomers and liberty bodices over our vests. I wore Tor's cast-offs. Nothing was bought if it could be made at home. No money had been spent on the tree in the schoolroom which was a stunted little larch, lopsided and half bare, dug from the garden. My sisters were on the floor making decorations from used exercise books, cutting the paper with careless speed. The carpet was covered with clumsily shaped dolls. Tor was trying to cut out a star. They had pushed bunches of grass and dead leaves into the tree's bare spaces. A lump of mud clung to the bark. My sisters took daily nature walks with Gov, to find specimens in ditches and fields. There was no holly or ivy in the room. One of them had tried to fashion a bell from a wire coat hanger. I gazed.

'Oh, Bonnie, it is beautiful. What is Bruno doing down there?'

Our baby brother was on the floor under the lowest branches with his head lying on a birds' nest. He wasn't wearing his clothes.

Nurse let out a scream from behind me. What had happened? Where was Maggie? Mercy. Maggie came up from the basement as Nurse called her.

'You filthy . . . What are you up to? The window open, he's not got a stitch on.'

'I'm only after fetching the cocoa for the two girls, Nurse. I left baby on the chair. It's those girls.'

'His death. He'll catch his death.'

Nurse snatched him. Bonnie and Tor watched from the floor. I had brought Nurse into their schoolroom, I had interrupted, I was trespassing. Then they shook their hair over their faces again, resuming their Christmas task.

Nurse rolled Bruno into his shawl.

'Come along, Ula. Straight upstairs.'

She'd never be able to trust Maggie again with him, poor lamb in the dirty leaves. Look, grass on his head even. I cradled Tin in my arms. I never had liked Bruno. I wished that my sisters had made that tree just for me.

There were rock cakes for tea in the nursery that evening. Maggie knew I liked them, made with jam. I ate my meals with Nurse on the top floor, my sisters ate in the schoolroom below. I ate my cake slowly; a little nest with blood in it. Maggie understood me. I wanted her.

'Nurse, I want another cake.'

'Well, you can't, Miss. Greedy. Sugar is bad.'

When she put her face close to Bruno's the world seemed to shrink, just Nurse and him, with me outside. And Bruno had a fever now, she said angrily, his forehead was all hot. If he caught a cold she'd see that Maggie was sacked.

He refused his bottle. While she was getting his nightdress from the bathroom I climbed onto the table to the cakes. I wanted another, I must have one. Even more, I wanted to disobey. Maggie mustn't leave us ever. I stretched my hand out to the biggest, so red, so pretty, so sweet.

'Greedy. Disobedient. Sneak thief.'

Nurse always punished me the same way. Straight to bed and no toys. She took away Tin. I sucked my fingers. I'd lost the scrap of silk from Lucy's dress. She'd been wonderful, she'd stuck her tongue out so comically. I must be like her, I must see her again. While Nurse muttered in the nursery about her lamb all cold and neglected under that dirty tree, I fell asleep thinking about Lucy.

TWO

'Talk to me, Maggie. Say something.'

I liked being with her so much, she understood everything. She knew what Nurse was like upstairs, and what Bruno had done to my life, though Maggie loved Bruno herself quite a lot.

On Sunday afternoons I stayed with her in the kitchen while my sisters played in the schoolroom upstairs. Nurse was almost happy on Sundays, she had Bruno to herself. Maggie never stopped working. There were trays to be carried up and down and all the cleaning. Mamma, if she was at home, ate alone too. Maggie's own home was in Ireland, a perfect paradise she said. The Irish loved children, I was her dotey love. She never went out at night-time, the weekends were her favourite times. She liked minding Bruno with my sisters on Saturday mornings, though my sisters weren't as nice as me. Gov was too lardy-dardy with them, Gov had made my sisters too superior to breathe. I liked pretending that Maggie was my mother while I listened to her talk of her home. England was godless in her opinion, and the way we were reared a disgrace. We lived miles from a proper church, we'd no religion. But for her we'd be truly lost. She let me play with her rosary beads, and sung hymns to me. She worried

17

about missing mass. Her immortal soul was at risk in this country. I loved listening to her talk.

'Is it my brogue or my clever thoughts you want to listen to? Did you enjoy the dancing class yesterday?'

'I met Lucy. She's my friend.'

'Lucy what? She'll be English, I suppose?'

'I had a dream about her, it was awful.'

'Awful? Was it a bogey-man? Just you press on that rolling pin.'

She baked crusts in the oven to flatten into breadcrumbs. I grated salt for her too. Another treat was to make mustard from powder, to put into blue glass mustard pots. I liked the smell of it and I liked watching Maggie working. She had a plain round face and straight hair. Her pink hair slide pinned her hair above her right ear. Her parting showed her greasy pink scalp. Short stubble grew on her neck. I longed to wear a pink hair slide but Nurse wouldn't let me. Everything I had was plain and dull. Lucy had worn a pink hair ribbon. Maggie had small sparkling eyes.

'I wonder where Papa went when he died, Maggie?'

'To the angels it is to be hoped.' She added that I shouldn't be worrying over such things, it was morbid. She would make a batch of scones for the tea.

I sifted flour for her and wondered if we'd get presents in a stocking at Christmas. In Ireland Maggie said no child was left out. Bonnie and Tor had worked hard with their Christmas tree. I thought Bruno looked better without clothes. Nurse disapproved of Maggie's cooking; too many eggs, too much sugar and jam. Maggie thought Nurse was old-fashioned, children needed a bit of sweet. I was alone too much. Nurse gave me nothing to play with. Was it a wonder I dreamed in the night? It was Maggie who had given Tin to me but I didn't need toys if I had her. As well as being in the kitchen I liked listening outside the schoolroom door. My sisters' nature walks with Gov sounded exciting. They wore wellingtons and kicked up the leaves. They scrambled up banks looking for lichen. Gov knew about fossils and stones. Nurse said they were wasting their time. When she wheeled Bruno outside I had to cling onto the handle of the pram. It shocked Maggie that none of us knew any prayers. She was extra worried about Bruno with his cold on his chest. Not that she blamed herself, she'd not neglected him, it was my two sisters who were to blame. They were bold and superior those two girls were, them and that funny-looking tree. In Ireland now all the trees were lovely, the one in their house was the best in the street. A good Christmas tree was like a good Christmas cake, a sign that all was well in the home. She'd miss the home-baking this year, thanks to Nursie. Imagine fussing over a bit of red jam. She sighed.

'Oh Maggie, you'll never leave us will you? Can I empty the bucket outside?'

A cobbled pathway outside the back door led to the dustbins at the end of the kitchen garden, where nothing was growing now. I walked across the stones carefully, holding the heavy bucket in both hands. The night frost hadn't thawed yet, the cobbles were slippery, the tree branches looked whitey grey. I was never afraid if Maggie was near me. There was frost on the lid of the bin. She was methodical about waste. Newspaper bundles of refuse were tightly wrapped, there was a separate bin for ash. I liked looking inside them. Nurse wouldn't allow it, she was prudish, I wasn't allowed to look at dogs' messes on the roadside, or even at myself without clothes. I would have enjoyed poking now into the packages in the dustbin, the old bones, the peelings and tea. Maggie called me. I emptied the bucket and replaced the frost-covered lid. The bare tree branches against the sky were like animal faces, birds with opened beaks and even a baby with close-set eyes. I envied Bruno, wrapped up and protected, but I had Maggie with her pink slide shining in the light. My hands were numb when I got in again.

'Feel them. Frozen cold. Put them in water now.'

She got a new piece of soap for me with a stiff outer wrapping and transparent paper inside. I liked the smell and the taste when you touched your tongue to it. I rubbed the lather until my hands were dry, rinsing them again to soapiness. I made bubbles between my forefinger and thumb, I rubbed soap onto Tin's hooves. The brown of his spots was the same as Lucy's father's coat.

'I wonder if we'll have presents under the schoolroom tree.'

'How can I tell you? I wasn't here last year.'

It seemed to Maggie that the English did nothing properly. Back at home Christmas was a fairyland time with presents, tree, lights and feasting. Nothing had been said about Christmas fare, she'd not liked to ask that lardy-dardy Gov. The housekeeping was a long way from being generous. That dirty old tree was a show. 'Course Ma'am, my mamma, was out enjoying herself in London. Things might change here if she'd return. But what Maggie found hardest to bear was the want of any faith, for which she blamed my mother and Gov.

'Can we look at your pictures now, Maggie?'

She kept magazines under a cushion for me to cut pictures from. She liked cutting them herself as well, particularly film stars like Boris Karloff with their slick hair and signet rings. I liked the ladies best. We gazed together at Mae West's curves and filmy clothing, we were in awe of the size of her behind. She said she had lollopers the size of twin balloons. Maggie's own lollopers were floppy and soft. I liked leaning against them as I cut out the pictures. I had never seen a film or a play. She said she'd bet Mae West had a lovely tree this Christmas and knew how to celebrate the holy birth.

'What birth? What do you mean, Maggie?'

She was horrified again. Did I not even know the meaning of Christmas, when our blessed Lord was born?

She spoke about the stable in Bethlehem, the wise men, the shepherds and star, while I cut out Boris Karloff's nose. I asked her what presents she'd had at her house. I pulled at the medal she wore round her neck, half listening. She said I should start learning to read.

Mamma had once seen me listening outside the schoolroom. She'd been angry. She paid Nurse to look after me, my place was upstairs with her, not listening at doors like a kitchen maid. Eavesdropping was an abhorrent practice, I would learn nothing to my advantage that way. She disliked children creeping about. Bonnie overheard Mamma and taunted me. 'Creeper, listening at doors.' I longed to be friends with my sisters, to share their sisterly world, but they neither needed nor wanted me. I wanted to learn lessons from Gov who wore tweed suits and sensible shoes, carrying a walking stick on the nature walks. Maggie got no thanks or appreciation for looking after the nursery as well as the schoolroom, carrying up trays and buckets of coal. She cleaned the nursery but not the schoolroom, Gov wanted no interference there. It stayed rather dusty and untidy, another source of Maggie's contempt. Nurse and she disliked Gov because she was not obliged to work, but came to us out of love for Mamma. She wasn't subservient. Gov had no religious faith and in Maggie's view was one of the world's worst. Maggie prayed daily to her guardian angel as well as her special saints, St Margaret and Our Lady.

'Have I got a special saint, Maggie?'

'St Ursula is a good saint. Were you named for her?'

'Ula. Not Ursula. Bonnie said Ula means owl.'

'Owl? Sweet Saviour, are you sure?'

Bonnie has been gleeful. 'Creeper. Kitchen maid. Owl.'

'Is it a fact? Are you a little birdy bones?'

I looked it, Maggie said: too solemn, too bony, a little bag of bones. She'd love to fatten me, to convert me, she'd love me to be her child.

'And you'll always stay, won't you, Maggie?'

She said she would unless Madam took a notion to leave. She might sell up and leave one fine day, you never knew. I would stay with her always. I leaned closer, her lollopers were warm. I liked listening. She complained about England, the unfriendliness, the gloom. They didn't laugh here, they hated babies, they didn't have any beliefs. She loved her old birdy bones though.

'Can we make jam rock cakes after the scones? Why has the man on your medal got a dripping bloody heart? Will you take me to Miss Dance next Saturday? I want you to see Lucy.'

She said that the other nurses wouldn't like her there, being too lardy-dardy themselves. Did that Miss Dance know the jig?

'What's a jig?'

Everyone should know the jig, she said. Watch now, she'd show me how.

She put me down, she took off her apron. Her cotton dress cracked with starch. She took her shoes off, pointing her right foot forwards, then both feet started to move. As they flew faster and faster they gave off a friendly smell. Damp patches showed under her armpits, widening as she moved. I sat on the floor by the table, she told me to hum the tune. The jig was called 'The Blackbird', her lollopers jerked in time. Soon the imprints of her black stockings showed over the tiles. Her pink hair slide flew into a corner, her belt buttons snapped and fell. This was better than curtseying and marching, 'The Blackbird' was fast and free.

'What do you think you're doing, Maggie? I can hear you from right upstairs.'

'Nurse. I never heard you come in.'

'That's plain to see. You woke the baby. You know he isn't well, he must have quiet.'

'I was only showing Ula a bit of a step. She wanted to see the jig.'

22

'Jig? Jig? Look at you. Button your belt. Mercy.'

'Aye, look at me, Nurse, and look at you. Is it any wonder Ula likes it downstairs with me. She gets a laugh and a cuddle down here.'

'You ought to call her Miss Ula, you're only the cook after all.'

'Miss? Very lardy-dardy all of a sudden are we not? No one is in a hurry to call you Aunt.'

Nurse's complexion went darker, she narrowed her dark-lidded eyes. She felt her lowly position and Maggie knew it. Nurse should be running the home and not Gov, who wasn't a relation and was very old. Nurse despised Maggie for being Irish, a below-stairs servant and lowly born. For her part Maggie pitied Nurse, an aunt by marriage without status or love. No relative would get such treatment in her country; no wonder Nurse was so sulky.

'Come upstairs at once, Ula. And don't make any more rubbishy cakes for her, Maggie. They're too sweet for so young a child.'

Maggie put her shoes on, she winked at me. If she only cooked what Nursie wanted it would be prunes and steamed fish for ever more. A kiddy needed a treat an odd time, her birdy bones needed love.

'Can I see Bonnie and Tor? I think they want me.'

They never wanted me but I kept hoping. I wanted to see their tree again. They were doing their homework for Gov, until Maggie brought up their tea. I hoped she wouldn't dance the jig for them, I couldn't bear to think that. I pressed against the schoolroom door. Bonnie opened it.

'Got you. Creeper. At your nasty tricks again?'

'Let me in, Bonnie, for a minute.'

She pushed her face into mine. Her brown hair smelled of leaves.

'You heard what Mamma said, you belong upstairs. Get away from our door.'

I looked past her shoulder. Tor was at the table, using a

black crayon, pressing the page hard. The tree still stood there, sad and curious, dabbed with mud and bits of straw. They had drawn their curtains early to be dark and cosy, they didn't need anyone or anything else.

THREE

Up in the nursery Bruno was asleep again. Bonnie had
called me nasty, but I wasn't. I leaned over his cot, near to
the fire. It was colder on the top floor, Nurse was getting
more shawls from the landing. I listened to Bruno breathe.
He was making a panting sound, almost grunting, then
from time to time a little cough. His mouth looked square
when he opened it, his gums were ridges of bone. His
tongue was as big as mine but whitish coloured. His breath
had a dry burnt smell. Nurse didn't like me touching him,
especially by the tops of his legs. It showed I was rude-
minded, she said, let baby have his privacy. Was his nappy
fastened properly? He wet a lot. His barking cough
sounded again. He didn't cry tears, nor did I usually. I tried
never to cry at all. He couldn't help being ugly and
unlovable, couldn't help being born at all. Nurse's black
eyes went juicy with love when she looked at him, his own
eyes were pale slits under invisible brows. The pulse in his
pate had the faintest growth of down on it, the delicate part
you must shield, the part where the brain throbbed.

'Drat my blood. Mercy. Take your hand from his head at
once.'

She often made me jump with her shouting. I tried to

stare and ask questions rather than show I was afraid of her. I said that Bruno was burning, he was coughing and sweating.

'It's not "sweat", it's perspiration.'

I was too much in Maggie's company she said, picking up her coarse turn of phrase. Bruno didn't even perspire, he shone. He was her shining innocent lamb. She looked closely, she listened, his cough sounded croupy. She knew all about a baby's ills. She'd send for the doctor to be on the safe side, though she was quite confident. Steam kettles were the safest for croup. She'd get a kettle now, when she went to telephone the doctor.

'I want Maggie. Can I go down?'

'You can not. Certainly not. Now don't touch him. I'll be back in a minute.'

'I want Maggie.'

'Then you must want. She's to blame for the lamb getting ill.'

'It was my sisters. They undressed him.'

'She left him with them, didn't she?'

Nurse pinched in the corners of her mouth darkly. I watched Bruno's face again. His nightdress smelled of warm milk and very faintly of flowers. If Nurse let me help her I might like him more. She went on muttering about Maggie being the culprit. And of course if Gov pulled her weight it might help. Those two girls were out of control, she herself was overworked what with me to supervise as well as the lamb. She patted his face with a towel. Steam from a kettle would ease him and plenty of warmth from the fire. She put more coal on, rattling the poker and tongs.

'And you can be putting yourself to bed, Ula. You can go without a bath.'

'Can't Maggie bath me? Could I bath with Bonnie and Tor?'

They often played at being mermaids, I could hear them, splashing and singing below. The nursery bathroom was cold with very bright lighting.

'Get along at once. You can't have Maggie. Just clean your teeth and wash your hands.'

I was seldom in the bathroom alone. Nurse liked you to do what you needed quickly without loitering. I liked whispering and playing with the taps and hated her hard fingers when she dried me with the towels. While she went for the kettle and telephoned I could stay in the bathroom and play. I leaned against the basin. Nurse didn't like dancing or Christmas trees, she was as miserable as a witch. I squeezed a long string of toothpaste, watching it catch in the light. I squeezed it along the edge of the bath, making nests in the corners, watching it glitter, peppermint bright. Where was Bethlehem anyway? What was the thing called myrrh? More peppermint white over the sponge next. I had toothpaste in my hair and in my nose. I wiped the flannel over my face.

'Hurry up in there, Ula. You've been quite long enough.'

'I am hurrying. What's the time?'

'The time? Time you were out. Don't forget to sit on the throne.'

'I did. I did.'

The seat was cold. I jumped off before I'd been. Nurse was particular about what you called things. 'Perspiration', 'throne', 'down there'. Maggie said sweat, lavvie hole and bottom. I loved her saying 'birdy bones'.

'Are you sure?'

'Of course I'm sure.'

It was best to nod, to pretend. She didn't see the tooth-paste in her concern for Bruno. I lay in the little bedroom listening to his dog's breathing and barks. My hot water bottle hadn't been filled. Nurse only cared for his warmth. Where was Maggie? Then I heard her talking. She had brought up a tray of tea for herself and Nurse. Maggie didn't bear malice for long. She pitied Nurse as well as needing her. I heard the cups rattle, the tea pouring, they

27

had drawn up their chairs to the fire. Maggie said Nursie was wrong to stifle Bruno, she shouldn't keep the babby so warm. Maggie knew a lot about sickness in young children, too much swaddling could give them a fit. Too much heat was worse than too little, the poor babby might take a stroke. Just as well to call the doctor she agreed, but she'd not harmed Bruno yesterday. The two girls were only having a bit of fun, she'd been below getting the cocoa. Fresh air never harmed a babby, letting the air to the skin. Of course those girls were unmanageable, that Gov was a lot to blame, had a lot to answer for. They were allies again, united once more against Gov. No one remembered my hot water bottle; I listened to the click of their spoons and the poker rattling against the fire bars. I wished that I'd sat on the throne. Nurse's rule was that once you got into bed you must stay there. She didn't allow fidgeting or calling, you stayed quiet until morning time. Maggie went down again. She didn't say goodnight or look towards my door. I heard Bruno's cot being moved. He had stopped coughing. I wriggled downwards. I wasn't comfortable or warm. I had a pain down there. Wanting to go made you shiver, making a smell could help. It cured the pain for a moment. Another one, Nurse would be cross. And another, you can't help it now, you must. Now I have done something awful, something I'm not allowed to do. Bruno does it, he's a boy and a baby, I've done something Nurse won't forgive. I will lie still and pretend to forget it, I didn't, I'm not dirty or rude. I will put my hand down, I've got it, a little sticky stick. A warm stick with porridge on it, now I've got it over my hand. Push it down onto the hot water bottle, smelling awful, push it all onto the floor. Rub my hand on my pillow. There now. Someone is crying in the nursery, a man is there. Nurse is crying, I don't know why.

'Now, Nurse, please, brace yourself. For the sake of the baby, please.'

'I can't. I won't. No.'

'Where is the children's governess? Are you in sole charge here now?'

Nurse's voice sounded different, she sounded crazy. Gov didn't sleep in at night-time, oh no, a being apart. Gov had the power and the pleasure, none of the work here. Madam Mamma wasn't here either. Oh no. She and the cook general had all the worry here and the responsibility too. She knew about sick infants, she'd had the care of babies all her life. She'd cared for Bruno's father once, she ought to know. Steam kettles and heat cured the croup. Mercy, he as a doctor should know that. She'd give any medicine he suggested, but don't, just don't take Bruno away.

'There isn't any choice, Nurse. The case demands hospital care. The boy must be hospitalized tonight, if he's to be helped.'

In a grave voice he spoke of the membrane of the larynx becoming inflamed, the high fever, the child's toxic state. He spoke of a possible tracheotomy and as he spoke Nurse started to scream.

'Nurse, I am going to the hospital now myself. I won't wait to call an ambulance, I'll take the child now in the car.'

I got out of bed, I went to the nursery. I saw Nurse's terrible face.

'I want Maggie now, Nurse. I must have her.'

'Go back. How dare you. Naughty.'

'Nurse, I must intervene. The child is frightened, she doesn't know what's happening. Here, come here, let me explain.'

'I must have Maggie.'

'Fetch the cook at once, Nurse. Stop making that noise. I will take the baby now.'

'She's not cook, she's my Maggie. I want her. I want Maggie now.'

He knelt down to me, he talked quietly into my eyes. He was a doctor, he knew about illness, he was used to fear and alarm. He was used to comforting children, explaining what was going on. I must understand that there was nothing to be frightened about. He was taking my baby off to be made better. Bruno was going to be cured. I looked at his kind face. I believed him. I wasn't worried about Bruno going, but of what I had done in my bed. I wanted to tell him, I think he would have understood, but Nurse was there making that noise.

'Is Bruno going to die, then?'

'He's very ill. He won't die.'

'He liked the Christmas tree in the schoolroom. Bonnie and Tor put him there. They made the tree. It's downstairs.'

'There'll be all sorts of fun in the children's ward. Don't worry, he'll get loving care.'

I was afraid that he'd think ill of my sisters. I wanted him to understand that it was Nurse's fault, she was no good with children or babies.

Maggie came up again, her hair was on end. She stood rubbing it with her hands. She'd been washing it below, had guessed at once that Bruno was bad. Her hands rubbed slower as she stood there, gradually they stopped. She didn't want to believe her ears. The little babby would be with trained nurses, white-coated doctors would stand at his bed. He'd be fed sups of caudle, thermometers would be inserted, oxygen, with him maybe inside a tent. No Nursie to give him steam from a kettle, or to swaddle him in wool. Who would love him in the hospital? Who would pray for him? Sweet Saviour, where would it end? I pulled at her. Maggie. Maggie?

'I'm here, pet. I'm here, Ulie. There.'

'The man . . . the doctor . . . he's taking Bruno.'

'I know. I know. All right, I'm here.'

Maggie talked quietly to the doctor. She was experienced, couldn't she take over? She knew about quinsy and diarrhoea. Did he have to take babby away with him? He

30

answered quickly in a low voice. Maggie shrugged and nodded her head. She'd be in charge, yes surely, she'd manage everything here. Nurse was too excitable, she was beside herself. Leave everything to Maggie May. She straightened her shoulders, Doctor could rely on her, she'd see the family through this trial. She listened closely while he spoke to her. Nurse was making too much noise to hear. Maggie took the pills that he handed her, she would see Nursie had one later on. He needn't fear, she would stay up here with Nurse and Ula while he took babby down.

Nurse sat at the nursery table, Bruno's nightdress held to her eyes. Her steam kettle, her loving attention and shawls hadn't saved him, her baby, her lamb, her love.

'Now then. Hop into your bed with you before I give Nursie her pill. Sweet Sav . . . Ula? What did you do? Your bed . . . Holy . . .'

'I didn't, Maggie. I didn't . . . it wasn't me . . .'

'Of course you didn't. It wasn't you at all. Ah God, Ula, the smell.'

She pulled the bedclothes off my bed, rolling them up, she got a clean nightdress for me, murmuring in a soothing way. 'Course it wasn't me that done it, 'twas that bogeyman all the time, and something to lay at Nursie's door. She was too strict with me, she bullied me. Imagine not letting a child to the lavvie hole. Maggie might be a coarse old peasant girl but she wasn't cruel like Nurse. A child should be let go any time, day or night. Poor little Ulie, with her baby brother gone.

'I want . . . I want . . .'

'I know what you want. You shall have it, so you shall.'

'Where did Bruno go?'

'With the doctor to the hospital is where. To the bathroom with you. Look at your hair.'

More Pears soap, more hot water, lapping under my chin. Maggie's soft rubbing hands were kind on me. There there, scrub my little bumbum, and a jug of water over my hair. I was her birdy bones and don't forget it. Lean back now. There. I wanted to stay cradled for ever. Warm water, sweet soap and sweet sound. She wrapped me in the big bath towel, her own clean hair close to mine. I was her dotey love, her darling, lean on her lollopers, don't be fretting. She'd need to see to Nursie next. The poor creature still in tears out there, she'd need to give Nurse her pill. After that she would take me downstairs with her, so don't go to sleep yet birdy bones in the big towel. Because I could tuck down inside her bed with her. I was nice and respectable again, clean as clean. There.

Tucked tightly into the far side of her bed by the kitchen I slept without feeling alone. The picture on the table by me was the same as the medal she wore round her neck, the man with a beard and thorns round his hair and his heart bleeding drops of red, the face Maggie seemed to love.

In the morning she wasn't there beside me. Maggie was upstairs in the hall talking into the telephone. This time it was she who was in tears.

FOUR

Hatred and suspicion of Gov had been Nurse's and Maggie's main contact. After Bruno left Nurse wasn't the same, she barely spoke. Maggie took over my care. It was she who told Bonnie and Tor what had happened. When I left Maggie's bed that morning they were standing in their nightdresses at the bottom of the stairs, their hair hanging in tangles over their disbelieving eyes. They wore the stern look of judges, weighing up what Maggie had said. Nurse was above on the upper landing, muttering. Steam kettles would have saved him, the doctor should have left him alone. Maggie spoke through her tears.

'Be quiet Nurse, nothing would have saved him, he was too far gone.'

'Be quiet yourself,' Nurse shouted back, 'be quiet the lot of you, it's all your fault.' Her voice trailed, she mumbled . . . must have her lamb. Bring him, must have Bruno.

Bonnie and Tor stood still. They didn't trust the world outside the schoolroom, with its uncertainty and change. I sucked at Tin's right hoof. I had hated Bruno because Nurse loved him. I'd been glad when his coughing face had been removed. No more square mouth and gaping gums opening at me. Now I wouldn't see him again. The change in Nurse frightened me. Had she gone demented, shrieking at Maggie like that? Bonnie spoke in a cold high voice. Where exactly had Bruno gone?

'Yes, where Maggie? I'd like to know.'

I allied myself with my sisters in disbelief, dislike and unease. Perhaps they would let me into the schoolroom now. How resolute they were. Maggie said Bruno had likely gone to Limbo, yes, Limbo would be his whereabouts now.

'Where is that? I never heard of it.'

Maggie said she wasn't surprised, seeing the lack of religion here. It was a wonder we'd heard of God even. Oh why had he not been baptized? She should have thought to do it herself. A splash of water, sign the cross. Now he'd be rubbing shoulders with heathen babies, for the want of being named.

'Yes, but where is Limbo?'

Near to heaven, she said, not actually heaven, but somewhere like. Unbaptized children went there, though they might escape it if the parents had the intention, if they'd practised the faith themselves. Bruno's parents had no faith.

'All right, Maggie, we don't want to hear all that. Where is it exactly?'

Maggie explained in a pious voice about Limbo being a place of waiting, while sharing the goodness of God, not equal, not the same as heaven. Bonnie and Tor were not impressed, nor did they care to hear. By asking questions they were delaying acceptance of the fact that Bruno was dead. Death was alarming, it happened to old people and strangers. Nurse was behaving dreadfully. Tor asked if Bruno would be able to talk now. He'd have company Maggie said, but not company of the best, only those who didn't know right from wrong. Her eyes were concerned and dry now. She thought it possible that lunatics might go there, as well as the newly born.

34

'What about animals?'
'And toys?' I asked.

Nurse shouted again. Stop filling our heads with lies. Such talk was poison. This made Maggie annoyed. Holy church couldn't lie. She had tried to make allowances for this family, but don't accuse her of lies. Tor said reasonably that Limbo didn't sound very pleasant, and no one could prove he'd gone there. When was breakfast? Nurse was still muttering. Maggie said she'd get one of the pills. When Nursie was quieter she'd fetch everyone a snack. No sense in the whole family arguing and shouting.

She came back with the sherry bottle, a drop for herself and Nurse and suitable at such a time. Bonnie looked stern again. Gov might not like it, Gov would be here quite soon. Well, all right, but she and Tor would have some too.

'I want some. Can I?'

Out of the question, Maggie said. Little children must not drink. Bonnie and Tor could have a taste, but nothing for birdy bones. It wasn't everyday you lost an infant. I could nibble some cornflakes instead. There now, in by that Christmas tree in the schoolroom, we could all go there and sit down.

The crunch of the cornflakes comforted me. Maggie gave me some water in a glass. I waited to hear Gov's key in the lock. I wanted to hear her walking stick being placed in the umbrella stand, the flop of her galoshes being removed. Gov would make life more stable again, she would take Bonnie and Tor for their lessons. After lunch they would go for their walk. She might let me join them for a little, while Maggie and Nurse settled Bruno's affairs. Maggie was sitting in Gov's chair, leaning back in it. Nurse sat by the empty grate. My sisters were on the floor at the far side of the tree. Nurse drank from a brandy glass. My sisters only had a little drop, they'd become giggling and boisterous just the same.

'Don't start now, don't be bold,' Maggie warned. Just

remember the occasion. I asked Bonnie for a taste, a sip. Please. She seized the cornflakes box, shaking it over my hair. Look at poor Creeper, out in the cold. Look.

Nurse sat in a private world, a world without Bruno now. Her face was dark and wild. Maggie wriggled her toes. She'd miss Bruno as much as anyone, dear little babby. But his passing had proved that she was important here, she felt more important than Gov. She could understand how Nurse felt, she could understand us girls. She would look after us, she would manage, was well able to run this house alone.

'Does dying hurt? Is it sudden? Or is it like going to sleep?'

Maggie knew all the answers, she was in her element, death was a pet subject of hers. In her own country they gave death attention. This life only lead up to it. What happened after death depended on what you did in life. If you were good you'd reach heaven eventually, after a spell in purgatory. If you were bad you paid. They had grand funerals in Ireland, with wakes in the departed ones' homes, with friends and relatives dropping in to pray and commiserate and a bite to eat and a drink for one and all. Food and drink helped a death in her country.

'Yes, but what is being dead like?'

Nurse made a noise like a growl. Tor asked if snowmen had souls, and what about ghosts. Maggie drew her chin in reprovingly. That was enough now. This family was beyond the light. Did we know nothing? It was up to her to enlighten us, or we'd be in danger of hell's flames. It was so different where she came from, her country could teach us a lot.

'Why did you leave then, if it was so perfect?'

Maggie went red, she was angry. Bonnie was rude, she spoke out of turn, she was impudent. She'd a good mind to pay her back. Maggie leaned forward with her hand raised.

'Have you all taken leave of your senses? Nurse, what is

going on?'

No one heard Mamma coming through the front door. She wasn't expected. We'd forgotten about her. I'd almost forgotten what she looked like until I saw her. Of course, Mamma was beautiful, standing in the doorway against the light. We'd have to tell her about Bruno. What a good thing we had Maggie, well versed in deaths, wakes and sad news. None of us were dressed yet, the schoolroom curtains were still drawn. Cornflakes were everywhere as well as dried mud and grass from the tree. How I wished then that we could be ordinary, like the children at the dancing class with ordinary parents who lived with us, instead of a beautiful mother who was never there.

'We didn't hear you, Mamma.' If Bonnie was afraid she didn't show it.

'Evidently. Please explain.'

'Madam. Oh M'am,' wailed Maggie.

Mamma appeared to shrink into her fur coat as if she'd like to shrug off the lot of us. She'd been good enough to employ her old governess and her husband's old nurse, why couldn't they perform their duties quietly? She had neither interest nor sympathy for domestic scenes. How negligent Nurse was. She'd evidently lost her tongue.

'Ma'am. Ma'am.'

She told Maggie to stop being repetitious. And why had she been hitting Bonnie? Why was she in the schoolroom at all? What were any of us doing? The room was like a bear-garden. Nurse made a low sound. Bonnie and Tor drew closer together for comfort. At the same time they wanted to laugh. Sorrow was burdensome. Were they too glad that he'd died?

'You see, Ma'am . . .'

'No, I don't see. I can see that you've all gone mad. Nurse, stop making that noise. Explain yourself. Bonnie . . . don't . . .'

Bonnie tittered. Her teeth showed sharp and grey. I

37

knew she was frightened, I wanted to help her.

'You see, Mamma. Something has happened, it's rather a pity really . . .'

I wanted to put it well, like a grown-up.

'Pity? What is? You're a pitiful-looking sight, all of you. Sherry? At this hour? Where is the infant?'

'He's . . . he's . . .'

'Fetch him. You shouldn't leave him, Nurse. What? . . .'

'Sweet Saviour . . . Oh Ma'am . . .'

'Cook, stop being melodramatic. Ula, go on.'

'You see, Mamma, Bruno has gone. He's not coming back any more. He's gone to . . .'

'Get up, Ula. Stop crawling about like a . . .'

'He's at Limbo.'

'Nonsense.'

Maggie spoke her words in a rush. She had woken early, hearing the telephone ring. She'd got up to take the message, the wee babby was with the angels. Only yesterday he'd been under that tree.

Mamma interrupted. Angels, Christmas trees, Limbo. Cook's imagination was beyond control. Put that sherry bottle down at once. Where was Gov?

'She doesn't get here till nine, Mamma. You see, when Maggie answered the telephone it was the hospital, saying that Bruno was dead.'

I guessed that Mamma was playing for time as Bonnie and Tor had, refusing to consent to the truth. In clear words I told about the doctor, about Bruno's cough and croup. Then Bonnie and Tor started giggling, leaning against each other, mingling their hair. They were as uncomfortable and confused as I was, they had each other. I wished we were properly dressed. I started feeling that pain again. I licked my fingers, pressing them onto the spilled cornflakes. It was important to collect every one. Perhaps if I went upstairs now I might find Bruno there all the time, coughing and gnashing his gums at me, having given the household a fright.

'Stop spitting and licking your hands, Ula. Nurse, you had better leave the room.'

Nurse stared, not moving, hating her. Mamma was to blame for everything. She had gone away, leaving her family, leaving the wrong person in charge. It should have been her, Nurse. She was a relative, she'd been treated with ignominy, she was these children's great-aunt. Gov was a no one. Then, hardly opening her lips, Nurse hissed, 'She-devil. Mother monster, mother whore.'

Mamma's red mouth shook a little, her pointed face went pale. She turned from Nurse, she ignored her.

'Cook, will you clean up this room. Get up from the floor, children, Go up and put on your clothes.'

Nurse left without speaking again. My two sisters went to dress. Maggie picked up the glasses and bottle. I stayed, picking up cornflakes and twigs.

'It is true. He is dead, Mamma.'

'Yes, yes. I quite understand. Why don't you go with your sisters? Why are you staring? Just go.'

I said that the nursery would be quiet now, with no Bruno. Did Nurse have to stay?

'What do you want to do about her? Stop staring.'

'I've got a pain. I had one in the night.'

'Children get pains. Tell Gov or Nurse.'

'Gov only looks after Bonnie and Tor. Nurse has . . . she's gone funny now.'

What would happen to his milk powder tins? Who would use his shawls and his pot? He'd been so ugly. I'd not even tried to like him.

Mamma had eyelashes like a doll. They didn't blink as she said sharply that I could hardly expect her to produce another baby to suit Nurse. My father was dead, remember? One corner of her mouth had smudged, like a tiny red scratch in the flesh. Her eyes were challenging me. I knew that we were alike inside. Mamma does what she wants.

39

She fights for it. I want to love you, Mamma. Why can't you stay? Why can't you look after us?

'I'd like to drink from Bruno's bottles. Can I?'

'I pay a Nurse to see to you. Ask her. Why do you stare?'

'Don't you like it at home?'

She was blunt. She had come back to collect some papers, some more clothes and to check on our well-being. She knew her duty, she would do what was necessary. Was I trying to take her to task? Did no one ever consider her point of view? Her life was far from idyllic.

'Bruno is dead,' I repeated.

'What a very obstinate child. And your hair. What is wrong with it? Does Nurse . . . has she done anything about it? Are you eating properly?'

'It's nothing. I expect it will grow out. Maggie says the English don't love children. Or God.'

She said that Cook was not only illiterate and whimsical, her ideas were subversive too. She paid Nurse to keep me upstairs.

'Bruno is dead. It's all women and girls here now.'

'I can't stay. Why can't you understand?'

I said that Nurse had loved him. Why had not she? She looked out of the window at where the schoolroom tree had once grown. She spoke half to herself. I was an uncompromising child, voicing what other people only thought. Why did no one realize that she'd wanted a son only because *he* had? Every man wanted an heir. Human nature, a son to bear the name. She had loved her husband with devotion, abasing herself to please. Each pregnancy they had hoped. First a girl, then another, the third seemed like an insult. Once more, this will be the boy. And he'd died without knowing his son. She had been left with all that burden, that responsibility which she'd created purely for him. Nothing mattered after that, no point in a life without him. There was nothing left to share without his presence. She disliked children, she'd had them for him. The boy was born, she'd not cared. Nurse wanted to come, she had done her a favour. Now was her chance to leave. Two retainers, both elderly, and that idiot peasant girl. They could manage without her, she could lead the life she'd once planned. Unwanted people longed to be wanted, they needed responsibility which she'd provided. Her own deepest need was independence, not to live through another's needs. She achieved independence of thought and action having made provision for the home. She had accommodated three lost souls who cared for her children. She had time now for herself. She turned. 'And do you know, Ula, if I hadn't married your father and had children, I might be famous now? I have always wanted to act.'

'Why did you?'

She said she'd adored, worshipped him, put him on a pedestal. A woman must have love. He'd longed for his son, that poor little boy. Too late, all too late.

'You realize Bruno is dead?'

'Dead? I can't accept . . .'

'Stay. Won't you, Mamma?'

She had come for some clothes, she repeated. She had enrolled at a school of acting. Three children in Sussex wouldn't prevent her. How strange to have white in my hair. Children grew, they would cease to cling. She disliked and discouraged clinging, we must learn to stand alone as soon as possible. What she had done, and would continue to do, was for our good. Nothing would stop her career.

'Are you glad about Bruno? Do you wish we had died too?'

The look she turned on me was worse than an actual or threatened smack. She whispered my name. Ula. I was insensitive, I was crude-minded, I was ugly. I would grow into a loveless young girl. How could anyone be drawn to me, or admire me. She had just lost her son. Get away.

She went to the telephone to contact the hospital. Later on she left again but this time she took Bonnie and Tor with

41

her. Moral support for the various signatures and formalities. My sisters looked proud and pleased.

Maggie explained the night's happenings to Gov when she arrived. Together they went up to Nurse. I stayed in the hall. I lifted the telephone receiver. 'Hello. All hail. Hello nonsense, hail lies.'

FIVE

'And so, Ula, I'm sending you off with Cookie. Don't you think that's a good idea?'

'When? Will Bonnie and Tor go?'

'Just you and Cook. To Ireland.'

Mamma said that my sisters were to go with Gov to her cottage. Poor Cook deserved a rest too; she'd been a tower of strength since . . . all this had happened. So, Ula, you can be happy, with your beloved Cook to yourself. Nurse was leaving, Nurse was ill, it was best that she left quite soon.

'Where to? Where will she go?'

Because Nurse hadn't spoken for days, not since she'd been rude to Mamma. She'd stayed on the nursery floor swallowing her pills in silence. Maggie waited on her. She was sorry for Nursie all right; because of Nursie we'd have to change our lives. Mamma couldn't bring herself to mention the funeral.

The night after Bruno died Nurse had howled in her sleep. She ground her teeth as well. Maggie had to shake her awake before taking me down to her bed again to be her dotey child, her own birdy bones, her hope. Mamma had quite changed her opinion of Maggie: the girl was rough, but a jewel. She relied on Maggie now as much as she relied on Gov. She'd be happy to trust me to her care entirely.

Mamma hadn't lost her temper with me again since the morning that Bruno had died, nor had I seen much of her. I wanted to know if she would be famous like Mae West, if she would put kisses on Boris Karloff's mouth. I went to her bedroom secretly to poke and pry in her things. She loved clothes. I smelled her flowers and her soaps, I looked in her cheval looking glass on the stand. Here she scanned her hair and her eyelashes, here she dreamed her golden dreams. She had no grey hairs; I checked her hairbrush entwined with dark auburn hairs. I looked at her rows of coats and dresses, linen, satin, silk. She had quantities of shoes with glossy heels, I tried them, my feet weren't much smaller. The gold kid sandals with thin-as-string strapping fitted me. I tapped up and down before the looking glass. 'If I hadn't married I might be famous. I have always wanted to act.' I rubbed some red onto my lips, stretching them. I too would have bosoms one day. She'd be angry again if she knew I'd been here. Spying. Creeping.

'How long shall I stay away? Does Maggie know?'

'Of course. I don't know yet how long. I'll discuss all that later with Gov.'

Mamma depended on Gov but she was bored by her. Gov was old, staid and dull. Mamma liked her bedroom best, trying clothes on, altering her hair and thinking about acting.

Nurse was given her notice to leave on the morning of Bruno's funeral. Mamma went up to her alone. I stayed in the hall listening. There was silence after Mamma had spoken. Then Nurse made a nasty sound. Bonnie and Tor left the schoolroom to join me. Nurse's wails upstairs increased. My sisters held hands, their free hands held the banisters. I took hold of Bonnie's skirt. We waited, our raised faces staring up. I noticed that Tor's clothes smelled a little like Maggie's clothes. Tor sweated when she was scared and I knew that they were like me inside. Then

44

Maggie came up from the kitchen. She said she hoped Nursie wouldn't become dangerous, some people went strange after a death. But not to worry, she'd look after us. Nursie had mixed blood in her don't forget, poor old person, she'd brought a lot of this on herself.

Mamma's face was paper-white when she came down. Her pointed mouth stood out darkly red, she didn't look at us but went to her room. Acting was probably easier than motherhood, you only had to think of yourself and get the words right. The noise upstairs continued. Maggie said again not to fret, she'd take the sherry bottle with the pills. Nursie mustn't go to the funeral, no telling what she might do.

We were dressed in our darkest clothes. Maggie's little eyes were calm. We would remember this funeral for the rest of our lives, the day our baby brother was laid to rest. The death of a baby was special, what a shame there would be no wake. It grieved her too that the service wouldn't be Catholic but she'd seen there was no lack of flowers. The little coffin was covered with blooms, with Maggie's red roses like a crown on his head. The bouquet from me and my sisters was star-shaped, Mamma's was a pillow of tiny white flowers. Miss Dance sent pink and white carnations wired cunningly, but nothing from Nurse who had loved him best.

Mamma's black veil covered her eyes, her cheeks showed theatrically pale as we all got into the car behind the hearse. Bonnie and Tor kept close together, I would have liked to have held Mamma's hand. As we moved from the house the nursery window was thrown up and a chamber pot flew out hitting the roof of the hearse. 'Drat my blood, take that. It's all you're worth, the lot of you.'

'Sweet Saviour,' Maggie moaned.

Mamma stared through her veil at the flowers in front of us. Bonnie and Tor squeezed closer. Later they would talk and laugh about the happening. Mamma said quietly that the woman must be out of the house tonight.

I never heard anyone say 'drat my blood' again, I never saw Nurse again. 'Poor old soul' Maggie said afterwards, packed out of the house like a dog, it was worse than morbid. She kept me with her downstairs, after the funeral, and nobody saw Nurse leave. I asked Maggie if she would miss her, why she didn't say goodbye to her. It would just make a bad job worse, she said. Nurse might put a curse on her, she was capable of it. Together we listened to her feet clumping down the staircase, the bump of her black leather bag. Never again would I feel those bony fingers washing me, never again feel her pulling my hair. No one waved or hugged or smiled at her. The door banged; she was gone. We could get on with celebrating Christmas now, Maggie said. And just as well we were all going away. Back home in Ireland there would be proper decorations, proper food as well as religion.

'Where will you go for Christmas, Mamma? Do you mind being left alone?'

She said my questioning and staring was ill-mannered. She was doing what was best for us all.

'I only asked what you will do.'

'Questions, questions.' Life continued, I would understand it better one day. And I was to remember that she had loved my father and for his sake had borne him a son. She was not deserting us, she was providing for us, let me never forget that. I knew she wanted me to be loyal to her, to admire and love her if I could. I smiled. She said that it was sad that my smile was rare. Had my life been so very grim? She had never heard me laugh.

'I laughed more before you came. I don't like you seeing my teeth.'

She murmured that they were a poor colour but I had good bone structure. Good carriage was as important as looks. I told her I would like to look like her, which pleased her. Learn to walk well she advised, with confidence, grace and pride. She hoped that Miss Dance had taught me something, she'd paid enough. She never wanted to see me or my sisters as we were in the schoolroom, undressed, unwashed, uncombed.

'But *how long* shall I be staying in Ireland?'

'I keep telling you, it's not arranged. Gov is too old to work for much longer. Your sisters will be going to boarding school.'

Would Gov be fired too when she wasn't wanted? Had Mamma a truly cold heart? She said I was lucky to have this chance of travelling. She'd heard tales about Ireland. A romantic island somewhat given to rain. It was to be hoped that Cookie wouldn't let me run barefoot, or get nits in that grey hair of mine. Remember Ula to smile with confidence and grace.

'Shall I be learning dancing there?'

She doubted if I'd find the equal of Miss Dance where I was going. No doubt some rustic antics went on. They were a picturesque people, particularly the peasantry, fond of leprechauns and beer. She wanted me to enjoy the holiday with Cookie. I must learn to stop looking so sad.

'She isn't Cook, I told you. Her name is Maggie.'

'Yes, I quite understand you. I'm simply doing what is best.'

'How do you know what is best? How *long*?'

She supposed I would eventually go to the same school as my sisters. Did I want to go to school?

I wanted to knit dusters and make a scrapbook with pressed flowers in it. I didn't want to learn to read. Mamma had no experience of school. Her childhood with Gov had been charmed. A shame that Gov was so old now. She'd do her best to find a nice school. I must learn to be less critical of my elders. It was her own business what she called her staff. Those in lowly positions, porters, waiters, cooks, were most frequently addressed by the work they did. People simply forgot their names. It was the custom and moreover gave the workers a little dignity, especially as their work often had none. They were subservient, they were expendable but useful.

'Is that why we never called Nurse "Aunt"?'

She was in another category, Mamma said quickly. No blood relative, her employment had been ill-advised. That behaviour from the upstairs window had been iniquitous. Mamma went silent. We wouldn't mention it again. My sisters would be leaving shortly. I would go after Maggie had cleaned up the house.

When I had waited in the hall with Bonnie and Tor I had hoped we might become closer, united by apprehension, but they hadn't changed. I didn't expect them to think of me when they had gone. I didn't mind so much now, I would be having a proper Christmas with Maggie in Ireland, I'd be wanted and needed, I'd be the only child there.

I watched them leave for the cottage in Shottermill. They went without saying goodbye. I watched them go out of the gate and down the road on either side of Gov, talking excitedly. Later they would sit round her fire, having gathered the logs and twigs to make it burn well. They would listen while she read them stories. Would they sing? Would they play Happy Families and Snap? They had no fears or worries about boarding school, they had each other, they could read and do sums. They had never been lonely or treated unkindly. They would expect to be treated at school as Gov did at home. What you expected you often got.

I went into the schoolroom for another look before Maggie got there. Soon the tree would be taken down. There was a faint spicy smell of the cloves that Tor had stuck into oranges to make pomander balls, mixed with a thick smell of old dust. Under a chair was a wooden knitting needle with a length of unravelled floorcloth. Gov liked all handiwork to have a use. Without my sisters the tree looked even more beggarly. Most of the foliage was shed on the floor. Maggie had asked me not to hang about being idle, she had the whole house to make clean. People who left muddles were selfish, someone else had to pick up the mess. The tree for instance was the height of rubbish, I'd see a difference in her house at home. They made a special fuss of kiddies at Christmas, as well as the old and the sick. Poor old Nursie, it was disgraceful, like a dog with nowhere to go. Not that she wasn't pleased Nursie had left us. But whoever would bury her when she died?

I went upstairs again. No nurse now to call me greedy or a sneak thief. All was bare and silent and clean. No coughing or wheezing or breathing, just cold wind outside rattling the window. There was a faint smell of floor polish and soap. I climbed onto a chair to reach into the top drawer of the tallboy. It was empty, my fingers felt cold. I felt something soft and woolly, a white woollen bobbled sock, last relic of Bruno, caught in the back of the drawer. I put it back and got down again. Bruno's cot had been taken away, and the mattress from Nurse's bed. The bedsprings looked sharp and ugly. My own bed in the little room had no bedclothes, and a chair was on it. The grate was empty, all the curtains were taken away. The cold and the emptiness wasn't the worst. This must be what they called the feeling of death. Maggie thought that though my Mamma had a right to do anything she chose, as she was the one paying the bills, still it was a wicked thing to run from your own children, worse than murder, and they needing love and care. Without Gov and herself we'd be right little lost souls. Gov, though lardy-dardy and lazy about dusting, loved the two elder girls. Maggie had no great opinion of actresses. She liked to cut out pictures of them but they were best left in books on the whole. A poor class of person doing a poor class of work. She didn't think you'd find many actresses in Ireland. Her people knew right from wrong. I heard her calling me.

'No sense in brooding up in the cold. Come now and give

a hand with this tree.'

I went round with a little brush, sweeping up mud and leaves. I found more knitting under the sideboard, tangled with swirls of dust. A trail of cloves lay along the skirting board, their cracked heads split from the stems. I sneezed. I had free access now to the room I had longed for. I was dismantling it bit by bit, removing the magic. Soon it would be clean and soulless as the nursery. Never again would I listen at the door, begging Bonnie to let me in. I would never hear them whispering, wondering if they whispered about me. Maggie threw open the window. You would think someone of Gov's education would be more particular. Now then, Ula, that tree.

We placed it on its side on a dustsheet, rolling it into a long tube. I walked behind as she dragged it downstairs and out to the dustbin, where it stood propped up alone.

Time now to be thinking of our own packing, she said. I wished I had something new to wear.

'Mamma,' I asked her, 'could I have a pink dress for Christmas, a silk one with rows of pleats?'

I knew she would say no, though she had so many lovely things herself. She said pink pleats sounded frightful, I already had my cream Viyella. Maggie could buy me what I really needed, no pink pleats mind, nothing frilled. Some heavy shoes perhaps, Ireland might be muddy. And a sou'wester for the Irish rain.

Maggie got me two jerseys as well as new shoes. She wasn't buying a sou'wester just to please Ma'am. We were going to the city, not the bogs out in the wilds.

'Say goodbye to your Mammy now. Look up there, she's waving, see?'

I looked up as we drove off in the taxi. I saw her pointed face and her thin bright mouth. Was she sorry now that I was leaving her? Did she have no misgivings or fears? She hadn't kissed me goodbye or even touched me. She was at the window where Nurse had thrown the pot. 'Take that, it's all you're fit for.' I wanted to love you, Mamma. I wanted you. Now you are truly on your own.

SIX

Maggie wasn't used to travelling. Her only previous trip had been leaving Ireland to come here. She looked forward to showing me the sights on our journey, she knew what children liked. My Mammy had no need to keep telling her to keep me close to her, she knew all about youngsters' ways. The two of us were off to have the time of our lives; anyone would think she wasn't fit. In Ireland each and every child was cherished. Cruelty and neglect were unknown. I'd be safer with her than in Buckingham Palace, I'd be her family's ewe lamb. She'd make certain that I put a bit of weight on, I was too skinny for my size. She had only tossed her head when Mamma had questioned her about the troubles, about the dark stirrings in the north of her land. The only trouble she expected for me to run into was that I'd be spoiled from too much fussing. Her parents were expecting us, she had written. They were lonely since she'd gone away. A child in the house would bring Christmas alive for them.

As well as keeping close to me Mamma insisted that Maggie should not influence me with any religious talk. She wanted us to be free thinkers, she didn't agree with church. Mamma agreed with Gov; countries that made too much of religion often ended with civil strife. Nurse, if she'd had a faith, had kept it to herself, and Nurse didn't matter now. So Cookie, Mamma had repeated, no praying or church-going for her child, who must grow up with uncluttered ideas. Cookie's beliefs were quite hysterical, stalwart though she was in adversity. Troubles brought out the good in some people, so mind now, no preaching, no idols, no hymns. The death of the baby, followed by Nurse going off her head, had put the household under enormous strain.

'You'll miss your mammy all the same, I dare say.'

I would like to miss her, I ought to miss her. Can you miss someone you don't properly know? I ought to want to stay and comfort her. I couldn't wait to leave. My sisters were happy with Gov in her cottage; soon I would be happy too. I waved up at Mamma's pretty face at the window. I took hold of Maggie's hand. She loved me, she loved having me, now we both had each other to ourselves. We were heading for God's green island to enjoy a real Christmas.

She had made a picnic for the journey. Maggie distrusted buffet-car fare. There were sandwiches of soda bread and oranges to suck, in case our throats became parched, as well as a few jam rock cakes for the boat. Maggie loved all children, my mammy ought to know that, she'd no need to tell her what to do. You got a right rough crowd journeying to Ireland now, she told me not to speak to anyone, some folk were apt to make free, especially ones that had a drink on them. We would keep ourselves to ourselves. She'd packed some magazines in her basket, and I had my old tin toy.

We were taking the mail boat across the Channel. We left home early to catch the train from London. At the entrance to the station I saw another tree. A charity tree, Maggie told me, in aid of a sick kiddy fund. It was undecorated apart from the presents dangling from it, tied up with glittering threads. More parcels were piled at the roots of it and a

53

placard that she read out. 'We always care this time of year; help us to care more.' She said not to stand gawping at it either, I'd be getting presents too if I was good. A man was playing a saxophone. Maggie said it was a Christmas hymn, hurry now or we'd miss getting seats.

I had never been in a train. It was so long I couldn't see the end. The platform was thronging with people with cases, the train windows were filled with faces. Most of them were men, of all ages, shouting and pushing their way. More cases and bags were in the aisles between the seating; there were rucksacks and coats in the racks. Most of the men were smoking pipes or cigarettes. Mamma had told Maggie to get into a Ladies Only compartment.

'The smell gets into my nose, Maggie.'

She said not to start annoying her, the train was packed but we had got a window seat. I'd get used to the smoke if I ignored it. She smiled at the man who had given his seat up. Very obliging of him. She didn't look at me as she spoke.

I hated the smell. I had seen Mamma smoking thin Russian cigarettes but no one else smoked at home. Maggie had always said what a dirty thing it was; she didn't seem to care now. There was too a greasy smell of empty crisp packets and a smell like old shoes, newly cleaned.

'Can I have an orange, Maggie?'

'The train hasn't started. Greedy.'

She had spoken to me just like Nurse. She peeled the orange carelessly, squirting juice over me, keeping her eyes on the man. She put a segment into her own mouth, chewing with mincing movements. The orange was a sour one, a pip got between my teeth.

'When shall we have to go to sleep, Maggie?'

She said we'd be having a lay-down on the boat, but I was not to keep fussing now. Her voice sounded different, telling me to look out of the window at my last sight of England before it got dark. Tomorrow I would see Ireland's green. She had spoken often of the colour of Ireland, the grass and the snow were brilliant. People said it was the wet weather and the quality of light. Maggie said it was a symbol of rightness, the Irish didn't neglect their souls. The Pope himself thought the world of Ireland, the land that had never lost faith. My first glimpse would show me, after England's soot and grime. Any churches you might find in England were nearly all of the wrong kind. You'd have to come to Ireland to see what she meant, the country that did things right.

I sucked my tooth with the pip in it. Would I ever see Lucy again, or listen to Miss Dance's voice? It was a pity I'd not kissed Mamma nor waved to her.

'Look, look, Maggie, another tree. A Christmas tree in that window.' We were passing sooty tenements, most of the windows were dark. Maggie ignored my pointing finger. She said I had Christmas trees on the brain. She was still looking at the man opposite who had given up his seat. He was holding a bottle. After having instructed me so firmly not to look at anyone, let alone stare or smile, she was looking and smiling at him. Her voice sounded silly.

'That's a ferocious-looking pet your wee girl has there. Is it a goat or a lamb?'

The man leaned and offered his bottle to Tin who I was holding on my knee. I thought him stupid; anyone should know a giraffe. Maggie giggled and shifted her legs. I had never heard her laugh like that, nor seen her cheeks look so red. He stretched to touch my cheek with his podgy forefinger. I saw that he had bitten nails. I wouldn't answer him. He was trying to interest Maggie by showing an interest in me. Because of him she was using that silly voice, as if she had swallowed something too hot. She said she would take a drink from him if he insisted, she didn't normally indulge. But Christmas was Christmas, the smoke in the air had a parching effect, didn't he agree? Plus a drink helped make friends and pass the time. Was he partial himself?

She hadn't taken the magazines from her basket. She only had eyes for him.

He proffered the bottle. And would her wee girl fancy a drop? Maggie leaned over and whispered. Not her own child, no, she was minding me. My father and my brother had died, she was taking me home to her family for the Christmas. She sniggered when she spoke my name. Imagine it, Ula, named after some sort of bird. Had he heard the likes of it ever? I felt betrayed, she was poking fun at me, she was laughing with one of the right rough crowd.

'Yes, please. I would like some.'

Maggie didn't stop him from pushing the bottle into my mouth, she did nothing to stop him when I choked. The drink had a dirty taste, my tongue burned, he pushed the bottle further. I gagged, my eyes watered, I struggled and Maggie laughed. Her giggles got louder, poor little birdy girl, getting a drink to herself at last. He saw what was happening, he got up, he pushed himself between us. He patted my back with his thick hand. His handkerchief smelled vile as he put his face near and wiped me. It was Maggie he wanted, not me. His eyebrows had greasy roots and were thick as lichen, growing outwards over his eyes. One of the hairs pricked my forehead. I smelled his ears and the smell of his breath. A drop more of the hard stuff would put hairs on my chest, he whispered. Named for a bird, was I? He could think of worse things than that. He liked birds himself, birds of all kinds, he liked them big and soft. He looked from the corners of his eyes at Maggie's lollopers. Maggie had the bottle now.

At the other side of the aisle were his friends, dealing a pack of cards. The cards made little flapping sounds on the table in front of them. Their cigarette cartons and crisp packets were pushed aside. Would they deal Mick into the game, they called over. Would his lady friend like a hand? Maggie answered in her new mincing voice. She never played cards, thank you, never played games at all. The eyebrow man laughed coarsely, digging his elbow into her. No games at all? Was she sure of that? He rolled a cigarette, offering her one. She was welcome to join his friends if she'd a mind to. He'd be happy here talking to the wee girl. Oh what is wrong, Maggie, what happened to you? You are smiling and talking to a stranger, you are holding a cigarette in your hand.

The men smoked their butts down to the length of finger-nails, cupping them into their palms. They forgot us when they started their game, they put money in a small pile to win. Good luck to Mick getting off his mark with the lady. They had their own bottle to drink.

Mick sat against Maggie now, pushing his big thighs close. His greasy brows, his coarse trousers and his voice offended me. How dare he take Maggie away? It was getting dark. I held Tin to the window. Mick laughed again. Was my animal looking for food now? Was he looking to munch the stars?

The journey seemed very long. The card game was finished; Mick's friends started to sing. Then Mick joined in and gradually the rest of them went quiet. He sang the hymn that we had heard earlier on the station platform, 'Oh come let us adore Him'. I thought I had never heard such beautiful sounds. The carriage stopped what they were doing, they stared, they listened, sitting very still. I forgot everything but the sound of him, forgot Bruno's death and Nurse getting mad in her head. I forgot that Mamma didn't want us. Nothing mattered except the song. The rattling train, the smell of drink and smoke faded, I was happy. I believed he was singing to me. I was going to a magic green land, where the people sang like angels and where every child was loved.

When I woke up next I was in a hard bed under a scratchy sheet. I was sweating, there was a bad taste in my mouth, there was a throbbing sound. I was in a small room in a bed fixed to the wall. What shocked me most was that I was still wearing my shoes. My feet felt bruised. I sat up. My bed was high, with another one underneath. There was a wash-basin with small taps and a tooth glass and a rack to put your clothes on.

'Mag-gie. Mag-gie . . .'

Her voice answered sounding muffled. Stop annoying her, she was only outside the door. She still sounded as if she'd swallowed something. I got down. I put my head to the door jamb and wailed. I banged my head, I made noises of sobbing though not real tears. I very rarely cried. I put my heart into pretended weeping, I rubbed my eyes to make them red. Please, Maggie, please come.

'Sweet Saviour, stop that racket, you'll have us put off the boat.' She pushed me into the top bunk again, tucking the narrow sheet. She looked even redder, her face looked itchy, her mouth was swollen now. She forgot to hug me or call me birdy bones. Her eyes were silly and strange.

'You must stay with me, Maggie, you promised not to leave me.'

'In a couple of minutes I will. Stop pulling at me.'

'I'll tell Mamma you left me alone. You didn't stay with me on the boat.'

'Ah God, Ula. What has got into you? You spoil my sport, you spoil everything.'

She half stumbled, then sat on the lower bunk, her grumbling voice sank to a whisper, she lay on one elbow, then lay back with her knees sprawled.

She kept her coat and her shoes on but she didn't leave me. She was quiet except for her loud rude smells. Then she started to snore. I knew now why Mamma had worried; it was because of the right rough crowd. You couldn't trust them, they had tried to take Maggie away.

A grey edge of light showed round the curtain covering the porthole. Someone was banging our door. The engine had stopped, there was no more throbbing. We must have got to Ireland now. I leaned over to look at Maggie. She was covered by her sheet now.

'Everyone off the boat now. Now please, passengers, everyone off the boat.'

Maggie's head wasn't visible except for a lock of hair hanging free. I pulled her sheet, her face was puffier, with crumbs in the corners of her eyes. She opened them, she looked blank. She remembered then. Going home. The boat. Mick.

'There's someone calling, Maggie. They want us to get off the boat.'

She jerked to a sitting position, then she got off the bed. Was Mick waiting for her? Was he looking for her? Wait now, Mick, she'd be out in a minute now.

'It's not Mick, Maggie, they want us to get off the boat.'

Her hair was in spikes, she looked older, her body seemed huge and sad, nothing like the Maggie who had danced in our kitchen, more like a huge clown. Why oh why hadn't Mick waited? Was I sure it was one of the crew? Where was he? She must get him, it was my fault for making that fuss. She should have stayed with him. Hurry, Ula.

'I must wash my hands, Maggie, you know I must. You know I have to look clean.'

I ran water into the small handbasin, I unwrapped the piece of soap. It was like a doll's washing place for toys and children. I was delaying purposely while Maggie complained. I repeated in a virtuous voice that surely she wouldn't want me to arrive in her country looking neglected? And look, she'd lost her pink hair slide. She clutched her hair, making it wilder. Not her lovely pink hair slide? We looked under the bunks for it, we crawled round the floor space. It was her lucky charm, she mourned. Her Da had bought it for her. I wanted to find it. With her hair proper again she might be the Maggie I knew, proud of me, wanting me, happy to be taking me to her home. She must forget Mick with the eyebrows, he was awful. Where was the pink hair slide?

We didn't find it. We pulled her sheets off. Maggie had a headache now. She peered up and down the passageway. No Mick. He'd such a grand singing voice. All my fault for nagging and interrupting. The two of them had got on grand.

'Your eyes have got yellow in them. Why don't you wash them?'

She told me not to be bold. I said he'd got horrid eyebrows and nasty trousers and I was glad he'd disappeared. She started to raise her hand to me when we heard more banging. 'Hurry please now, passengers, last call.'

She asked the steward if he had seen her friend at all, a curly-haired man on the stout side, with a grand singing voice, travelling with friends. He said that everyone was with friends this time of the year and a good many sang as well. In the bar had her friend been?

Maggie took my hand again. Ah God, life was unkind to her. It was also very unfair.

'I'm here, Maggie. I help you, don't I?'

She had no man, she said, to support her, no kiddy or home of her own. She hadn't much money, nor the world's prettiest face. She'd not complained, tried to look on the sunny side. Meeting Mick had been a gift in her hand. Where was he? What happened? Where was the man with the darling voice?

I told her how much she had changed when he'd come. She didn't even sound the same. Didn't she want me any more, now she'd found him?

'I do, Ula. Oh I do. It's just . . .'

'What is it? Tell me.'

She said that she'd like me *and* Mick. She never seemed to get what she'd really like, very little went right in her life, she seemed to have lost her luck.

She searched again in her basket for the hair slide. We couldn't see Mick anywhere.

SEVEN

The streets looked drab in the dawn light, with the shops still shuttered and dark. There were few people on the wet pavements, moving quietly in their shabby coats. Most of the women wore headscarves knotted under their chins. The men had newspapers rolled to keep dry; the sports pages were precious. They paused under lamp-posts to confer with each other, their breath forming steam round their heads. I could see little colour anywhere. I looked for grass or a tree, even an empty flowerbed. There were no spaces even for weeds, only low buildings with broken doorways under the fanlights in empty narrow streets. Small shops on corners had lit windows. Some of the women pushed babies in prams.

'It must be cold out for a baby. Where are the gardens?'

'Don't mind these parts here. This is the outskirts.'

'You said it would be green. I just wanted to know where. I can see a green letterbox.'

She pointed to a church with people, mostly women, going in and out. There you are now, just as she'd said, people living right, observing the faith. See the statue of Our Lady, see the people blessing themselves. The men with the newspapers lifted their caps as they passed. A holy country all right, there was proof. Holy God lived in the churches, they were proper churches here.

'I know, Maggie, you told me. Where is the green?'

'Stop annoying me. It's early yet. You'll see plenty of green soon.'

She wished I'd drop my habit of pestering, it was a torment so early in the day. Ireland was as green as a parable, she could promise me that. Meanwhile she was hungry, she hoped her Ma was making a fry. She didn't mention Mick again.

Our taxi stopped at the end of her street outside another church, her church, she wanted me to see. Behind the railings and iron gate was a crib under a thatched roof with figures standing round a manger. There now, she pointed to it. See the beasts standing waiting, the camel, an ass and the lamb. See Mary and Joseph's pleased faces. I saw that they were looking down but no baby was inside the manger, only artificial hay.

'Has the baby died already then?'

She said I was morbid and heartless and no wonder, that was what ignorance did. The holy child would be there by the morning, He'd get born at midnight mass. The priest would come out of the church and lay Him down there in the hay. We could start Christmas then. See Our Lady's happy expression, see poor St Joseph's faithful eyes. She'd a particular devotion to St Joseph, Maggie had.

'Why?'

'Never mind the why. See the goat hiding in the corner?'

'Can I come to midnight mass?'

She said I might if I stopped pestering and tormenting, and I wasn't to annoy her Ma. Her Ma wasn't at all strong in her head these days. Understand, Ula? Look now, there was the green. Green grass growing all round the holy family. Satisfied? I didn't tell her that the grass was just green raffia like the mock hay in the crib. St Joseph had raffia hair, their faces were lumps of clay, but I wanted to see the baby getting born, let Maggie think it was grass. She pointed out the star on the crib roof, the star of Bethlehem pointing down. Mind, she added, Christmas wasn't just presents and excitement, it was praising the holy child. She looked sincere and tender, her face was less puffy now, as if she could see into the future. Perhaps she could see me being accepted into her church, with herself as godmother standing near. That mamma of mine had much to answer for, neglecting her children for her own pleasures, leaving them to others' care.

We walked down the street of terraced houses, which seemed even shabbier than the ones we had passed. Slates were missing from the rooftops, windows were boarded up with tin. The front doors opened onto the pavement, each one had a single stone step. Few of the windows had curtains. Maggie's door was battleship grey. The Christmas tree in her window shone out like a beam of light. The panes were sprayed with frost to which cotton wool blobs adhered. I looked in. Red and green paper chains twined from lanterns, tinsel whorls were tacked to the walls. The tree was immense, with spun glass birds on the branches. The top branches pressed the ceiling. A bird with blue and yellow wings was arranged as if swooping, its opened beak stretched to the door. The tree almost filled the room and the foliage was barely visible under the thick tinsel twisted round it. Coloured streamers hung from the small lights which kept flashing on and off all over it. I kept very still as I gazed at it. This was a real tree. I stood on tiptoe to see more of it. The bottom branches thinned into dwindling roots which stood in a bucket weighted with stones. There was no carpet in the room or any furniture except for a card table spread with newspaper. It was worth coming to Ireland just for Maggie's Christmas tree. I wanted to stay and look at it for hours. The grey door opened.

'Don't stand there gawping outside, Maggie May. You'll have the neighbours wondering again . . .'

'I've brought her. This is Ula, Ma.'

'I see her. I have eyes in my head, haven't I? Don't be standing gawping out there.'

The Ma had been watching out for us since first light, she told us. Whatever had kept us so long?

'Don't fret yourself, Ma, aren't we here now, safe and sound?'

'That child's hair, what is wrong with it? Come inside before you're seen.'

Maggie explained to her mother that my hair had been like that since birth. She couldn't help it, it wasn't her fault, whitey patches from a baby.

'Well come on in then, child.'

The mother pulled me from the window. This street was nosey and the family were proud here, they liked to keep themselves to themselves. I was already frightened of her, I hated the feel of her, there was something strange about her hands. She caught me by the point of my chin, peering closely at me with eyes that didn't look straight. How old was I? Was I a good child? Her hands felt like cloth on my skin. She had a short body on stumpy legs and her hair jutted out in a fringe over her unfocusing eyes.

'Leave her now, can't you, Ma?'

'Giving out the orders again, are you? And you scarcely over the step.'

'Ah, Ma. Stop.'

'Was life not what you hoped the other side? Did you not get yourself a man?'

'*Ma.*'

'Decided to honour us again, did you? It's a wonder they spared you the child. I've been on my own waiting.'

'I like your Christmas tree very much. Why isn't there any star on the top?'

I hated them quarrelling as soon as they saw each other. I must make the Ma want me.

'Well you may ask. I couldn't reach is why. I've not had

64

any help.'

'I'll put the star on, Ma. The boat was late. The crowds were fierce, we were delayed getting away off the boat.'

I wondered why she didn't mention Mick. I was glad that she hadn't. Maggie explained about the lost pink hair slide, the one which had brought her luck. She'd need to buy another later. She pushed her hair behind one ear. We had searched for it, looked everywhere, we were worn out from lack of sleep. Was the back bedroom ready?

The Ma stared, her little cross eyes looked worse. England had given Maggie notions all right. 'Is the back bedroom prepared' indeed. Would milady like breakfast in bed? Would the whitey-haired child like its bum wiped? Was it able to lie its own alone?

'Hush, Ma. Don't.'

Maggie said something in a low voice, about my brother and having no Da. And we'd neither of us eaten since last evening.

'You wrote about the wain dying, Maggie May. I heard it before.'

'Maggie, where is your father? Isn't he here today?'

The Ma answered before her, drawing her chin back so that it made one line with her neck. Nosey too, was I? One of the curious kind? English wains were good at being nosey, she'd heard.

'I just wanted to know where he was.'

She told Maggie to take me upstairs, and then come on down for a wash. The house felt colder inside than it had been in the street. Their staircase rose steeply from just inside the grey door. The back bedroom was opposite, at the top. It was barely bigger than the bed inside it and had a stuffy smell. It smelled worse than a zoo, Maggie said, opening the window. She forgot the broken sashcord; to keep it open it had to be propped up. She put the alarm clock under it and the cold air blew in on our hair. There now, did I think I could sleep in this room? With Mick forgotten and out of her mind she looked at me in her old way. I didn't mind the cold or the bare floorboards and the smell. This was Maggie's Irish home.

The room faced the back, overlooking the cracked chimney cowls and grey roofs that made a jagged line against the sky. The back yards were crammed with dustbins, old broomsticks and bicycles. A tin tub was hanging in Maggie's yard from a hook in the broken fence. A cat ran along the fence, jumping across the gap. A woman's voice called sadly, 'Tibby, Tib-bee.' Apart from the nail on the back of the door there was nowhere to hang our clothes. We would leave them in the cases and push them under the bed. Her curtains were pieces of sheeting tacked over the window-frames, trailing now onto the floor. The nails in the boards had their heads beaten sideways, the small heads scratched your soles. Draughts blew through the spaces where the floorboards ended and the skirting boards began. A dream of Maggie's had been to buy a red carpet to send home in time for the Christmas. A bare bulb hung in the hall. I saw no other lights except the Christmas tree ones. Maggie said I needn't start pestering to use a bathroom because I'd just have to use a po. The lavvy hole was out in their yard, that was all there was. So, po or brave the cold again? All I wanted was to go downstairs to where the tree glowed rich and rare. I could hear music playing. She said it was Ma's wireless set, she listened to it all day long.

The kitchen was under the back bedroom and was where the family spent most of the time. On the end of the draining board was a huge wireless in a heavy wooden frame. The control knobs were set in a design of silk pleating with wooden spokes like a fan. Maggie's Ma stood watching the wireless with a fixed look, her lips moved to the words of the song. She turned.

'Stop staring with the big eyes of you. Get washed, English wain.'

'Where?'

At the sink, of course, she told me. This wasn't Buckingham Palace here. They were plain folk, plain living and
plain behaving. What water they had came from the sink.
Nor would I get waited on while I was here. Maggie had
told her all about that nursery of mine, with the trays up
and down, the bathing and fuss. I'd have to come to earth
here in this place, I'd get no special treatment here. There
was the towel, get washed English child.

'I like your wireless a lot. I like your house as well.'

She looked pacified. Did I like Henry Hall? I said I
thought I did, though I'd never heard of him. We had not
had a wireless at home. Mamma being rarely at home
hadn't needed one. Gov thought it an unnecessary modern
invention. Maggie's Mullard Long Lasting mains wireless set was the love of her heart. Her little cross eyes stayed
wistfully watching it. Next to Henry she loved Joe Loss. She
broke an egg into a cup before tipping it into a frying pan.
The gas jet burned high under it. She added some lard.

'Mind Ula's clothes, Ma. That jersey she has on is new.'

It was a fawn jersey with pink stitching round the neck
and the sleeves. Maggie had chosen it when she bought the
shoes. I didn't think Mamma would approve. The Ma put
down the frying pan angrily. Let Maggie cook the breakfast
if she was so particular, she'd sit down and eat her own.
She forked the egg onto her plate and sat at the draining
board to eat it, leaving Maggie to cook for me. She ate
slowly with quivering movements of her jaw and neck,
keeping her eyes on her set. Eating increased the pleasure
of listening. She hardly blinked as she ate.

The scullery was barely wider than a passage, with the
sink, the gas stove and the draining board down one wall.
To get to the lavvy hole in the yard you had to squeeze past
anyone in the scullery. Meals were eaten at the draining
board, where bread, eggs, meat-paste jars and a tea tin
were kept. There was one shelf for cups and plates.

Maggie fried my egg, not burning it, spooning the fat

onto it so that the yolk set with a milky-looking sheen. I'd never eaten a fried egg, only boiled ones. She cut it into a cup with squares of buttered bread sprinkled with pepper. I sat beside Maggie, all of us waiting for Henry Hall. Their spoons tasted like hot pennies, but I still loved the taste of the egg. I would be quiet, grateful and appreciative, I would make them want me there. The lavvy hole had a seat like a plank over a hole. The toilet paper was squares of newspaper pushed onto a nail in the wall. Come back in quick, the Ma shouted, or the whole street would be talking. Maggie should have put something over that hair of mine. That queer patch of white was like nit eggs.

'I don't like wearing hats, actually.'

' "Actually". This isn't "actually" England. The family is well thought of here.'

The Ma turned back to her wireless set and the signature tune of Henry Hall. Maggie told her that she would take on the cooking now, and the housekeeping. We'd buy anything we needed now.

'I wonder if there'll be presents tomorrow, underneath your tree?'

'Wondering and wanting, a true Englisher you are, on the lookout for your gain. You didn't bring anything yourself, I'm thinking. You'll be quick enough to take what you can.'

I wished I had something for her. I wasn't used to giving presents, I had never been given pocket money. Even a duster knitted by Bonnie would have been something, or one of Gov's pomander balls. Presents were something you dreamed of and hoped for, but didn't often get. The best present I'd ever had was Tin, from Maggie. I didn't know why the Ma hated England so.

The father was in the fuel trade, delivering logs from door to door. He handled Christmas trees too at this time of year, but not turf. The men in the turf trade were apart. He'd be late in tonight, he'd be kept working, it was the same every year. Their tree in the front room had been the biggest he could carry, it had taken two men to get it in place. The trees came from the country, where the Ma had lived when she'd been a girl. She had met the Da twenty-odd years ago when he'd been loading wood for the city. Her part was the greenest county of Ireland, full of lakes and wooded hills.

'How is his lordship anyway?' Maggie's voice sounded sharp.

The Ma said he was middling; some people never changed. And was there something wrong with my teeth as well as my hair? You'd not believe I was an English nob's child. Her woolly-feeling hands grabbed hold of my chin again. Her breath smelled of olly filed egg.

'There's nothing wrong with them. I have strong teeth. Grey teeth are made to last. Maggie told me.'

I wished she would let me alone and stop criticizing. I tried to cover my teeth with my lips, but I knew I ought to smile. If you smiled people treated you well.

Maggie said we'd get ready now and go out for the messages. There was nothing in the place fit to eat. She asked the Ma if she should get a bird or a joint of spiced beef?

'Please yourself, Milady. It's you that will be doing the cooking.'

The Ma added that it was all the same to her, she wasn't rightly fond of meat, and to make sure and cover my hair if I was going out.

When we were in the street again Maggie told me not to heed her Ma. She couldn't help her nerves being bad, it was her time of life. Nerves made a woman snappish, but as long as Ma had her wireless she wasn't any trouble. I was too busy looking at the trees in the windows to listen. They were all sizes, from doll-sized trees in saucers trimmed with silver thread to trees filling the windows. Some of them were made of tarnished tinsel, brought out and used year after year; others were real and splendid, but Maggie's was the best. I ran from window to window along the length of her street. Look, Maggie, look at that one, but she didn't seem to care.

We paused outside her church again to look at the crib. There would be singing here tonight, with candles and praying. All the families in the street would be there. But hurry now, Ula, we had work to do first. There was the Christmas dinner to buy and prepare, not to mention the tea afterwards when we got in.

We chose a capon. Stuffed and cooked rightly, Maggie said, a capon made as good a dinner as any else. She liked stuffing and basting a nice little bird, with a few sausages round it for luck. We chose chunks of white pudding to have for this evening's tea. A fry was lovely this cold weather, though strictly speaking the day was one of abstinence. She'd make jam rock cakes if she'd a minute to spare for afterwards. Did the butcher have black pudding by any chance, black pudding went down well with white. He looked at Maggie and winked at her. He'd plenty of the other out at the back. Would she come in and take a look at it?

Maggie started tittering and getting her silly look. It was happening again. She had met a man; soon her voice would change.

'Oh come on, Maggie. Let's go.'

'That's a dangerous-looking animal you have. Will I cut him up too for your tea?'

The butcher stretched his hand out to take Tin from me. This had happened before too. Men used Tin as an excuse to talk to Maggie, whose eyes had gone runny again. A man was there, and she didn't need me. When he leaned over and whispered to her, I smelled whisky again and Maggie guffawed. Ah well, Christmas was Christmas she said to him.

'What did he say, Maggie?'

'I'm telling your Ma that I've a pudden hidden inside, as big as . . .'

He made a gesture. I saw that his trousers had a bump in the front.

'She's not my mother, she's . . . Maggie. Maggie, we'd better go.'

She looked angry again. Was I interfering again? Killjoy.

'You said you'd make rock cakes.'

The butcher made another attempt. A slice of cake and a cup of tea would go well with him as well. Could he get an invite?

'Maggie, I need to go to the bathroom. I need to go now.'

She looked really ugly then but we hurried off down the street. At first she wouldn't speak to me, but we had the capon safely wrapped in newspaper. She did love making nice meals. We stopped to buy tangerines bundled into red netting bags, tied with red ribbon. We looked at a pile of apples, their red skins shining from tissue paper nests. An apple after a dinner cleaned the teeth, she couldn't resist telling me, and her eyes started to look natural again. She asked if I liked ginger nut biscuits, a favourite of Ma's with tea. She liked dipping and sucking them, poor Ma did. Still, she'd made a good job of their tree, her suffering with nerves and change. Ah, Christmas in Ireland was grand, wasn't it, Ula? God's own dear land of green. What she'd missed most away from it was colour. England was such a drab land. Our house had been drab, all those grey and brown shades and Ma'am never at home. Ma'am looked after her own wardrobe all right, oh yes, Maggie had never seen the likes. Ball gowns fit for royalty, to make no mention of those shoes. But she'd never seen kiddies dressed like we did, those nasty liberty bodices over our vests, and two pairs of knickerses, those drab old jerseys and skirts. Being away made her appreciate home more. Green grass and bright blue skies.

'The sky isn't blue, Maggie, it's grey. I've not seen any

proper grass.'

She said the reason for that was the snow. She'd heard snow forecast on Ma's wireless set. I'd understand what she meant when I saw the snow. The weather was dull just now, the snow would change everything. Irish snow was pure as chastity, a sparkling sinless white, and then the sky would be blue.

She made my home and country sound drab and spiritless, on an equal with our lives. She was generous with her money, she'd paid a lot for groceries today. At home with us she had sent money back to Ireland regularly. I felt ashamed again that I'd no present to give.

Maggie was staring at some flowers that a woman on the kerb was holding out. Weren't they beautiful? Roses for love. Red paper flowers cunningly twisted by gypsies and perfect in their way. She said the gypsies were bad people to cross, especially at Christmas, but she'd spent all her money now. I wished I had some to buy a rose for her. The woman spat after us. Maggie crossed herself. She'd already lost her lucky hair slide.

Now what about the lavvy, she asked me, did I still want to go? She might have guessed I only wanted attention, I could wait now till we were home. Here, take one of the apples to munch on. When I bit into the red skin the flesh was soft. Maggie bit into hers and it was brown. No matter, she said, she could make apple cake from the good parts; her Ma was partial to that as well as ginger nuts. And don't start on about rock cakes again, she would do what she could in the time. I didn't mind anything as long as I could keep her away from men. Men made her go silly and talk uncomfortably. She was still my Maggie with the greasy hands and hair who cooked nice things just for me. I said earnestly that I'd help her. I would be her right-hand man.

We heard the sounds of the Ma's wireless from the street outside. Maggie stooped, she called through the letter box. Hey Ma, we're here, let us in. The newspaper bundles in

her basket slipped, the capon flopped out onto the pavement, tangerine oranges rolled into the street. Blood had
dried on the beak and neck of the bird, it gazed up with
half-closed eyes, its yellow claws curled inwards. I tried to
get the newspaper over it again, the curled claws kept
slipping free. The bird had a slimy feel. Maggie picked up
the oranges. Hurry, she told me, there was a lot of work
ahead. You got a bird cheap if it wasn't cleaned, and cleaning it took time.

'Ah Ma, there you are. We're back. Is his lordship not
returned?'

The Ma looked frightened when she saw blood on the
newspaper. Blood at Christmas was bad luck. Maggie told
her to go back to her window again. We'll tonight white
pudden for tea.

The air was soon filling with the lovely smell of it. There
were thick slices of fried bread as well. Tomorrow we
would be spreading a cloth over the card table and eating
our dinner beside the tree. My special job would be cleaning the cutlery. I licked my fork, tasting the last of the hot
penny taste. Ma suddenly leaned over and grabbed my
chin again. What sort of a Christmas was I used to? What
did that nurse and that governess do? Did they not take a
holiday even at Christmas? Did we not eat together even
then? Maggie said it was England, Ma oughtn't to forget
that. It was a sad country that looked on everything differently. I said nothing, I couldn't explain that we lived
separate lives always, that what I liked best about here was
being together, eating cramped up from the draining board
near the sink. No more Nurse and I on the top floor with
my sisters down below and Maggie in the basement. This
was real family life here. I looked forward so much to
tomorrow's capon beside the flashing tree. The white pudding tasted as nice as it smelled, eaten with HP sauce
spread into the fried bread. I poured another brown blob
from the bottle, smoothing it with my knife.

'Here's himself at long last,' Maggie said, opening the oven to get out a plate of fry for her father.

'Maggie, me darling, it's my own Maggie May.'

He smelled as Mick and the butcher had smelled, a sour drink smell mixed with smoke. He had the same friendly watery eyes with crumbs in his eyelashes and his large ears stuck out each side. In spite of the look of him I trusted him, I knew that he would be kind.

'So this is the stranger. You're welcome to the house, stranger child.'

I liked the straight hair covering the tops of his ears and growing low on his neck at the back. He bent over me to kiss me. The Ma sniffed loudly; nobody bothered about kissing her. I didn't mind the Da's smell or his eyes; he looked me in the face when he spoke to me. I knew he was glad I was there. I liked the kind way he touched my arm, I had a place in his home, more than welcome. Had I had an easy trip?

'Get you to the sink now, Da. Your tea is overcooked.' Maggie poured the sauce over the pudding slices, reclosing the oven door. Ma turned her eyes back to the wireless set. 'Oh come let us adore Him, Christ the Lord.' The Da whistled as he squeezed past us by the draining board to get to the yard. When he came back he was ready to wash. I had never seen a man wash himself. He rolled up his grey cotton sleeves, bending his long back over the sink, turning the tap on full. Cold water flew from his hair. He washed with kitchen soap, huffing, splashing, spitting. When he stood up again he was changed, his skin shone clean and pink, his scalp glowed through his white hair. When he had dried his face his eyes were clear. He had thick white even teeth, smiling at me, asking if I'd seen the tree. Maggie said he'd be of more use helping to decorate it than staying out to this time of night. Poor Ma had done it alone and couldn't fix the star.

We sat in a row at the draining board, eating and listening to the music. When the news came on the Ma turned the sound knob down. No one wanted to listen to the world's troubles on this particular day. It was teatime on Christmas eve with white pudding and HP sauce. Maggie said I'd been such a help to her, carrying the messages home, helping to get the tea, she'd let me come to midnight mass. I wasn't one of them, the Ma said sharply, I had no place in a Catholic church. Let her, the Da said, there was room for all at this time, no matter how misled or wrong thinking.

Later on we all left the house together, but Maggie walked in front linking arms with her Da, leaving me to walk with Ma. Had it happened again already? Had Maggie forgotten me for another man? The street was thronged with neighbours all heading towards the church. Most of the women carried missals and beads, some held tightly onto their men who were not walking very straight. Everyone had but one thought in mind, to get there in time for the birth, to see the holy child placed in the crib. It was more serious than play-acting, the doll-baby would be blessed, a moment to love and look forward to. As we all walked along the neighbours noticed me too, the stranger child over from England, under Maggie Mullen's care. Ma whispered to me not to mind them, they were nosey, let them stare. She had made me pull my beret down low to cover my hair, the way she wore hers. Her unfocused eyes glared at me from under the navy edge and short tufts of her fringe.

A thick crowd waited at the railings watching Mary and Joseph who waited for their child. I heard someone ask if Maggie was home for good now, and who was that English child? I pulled at my beret self-consciously; I wasn't Catholic and I was named after some sort of bird. Then we heard singing inside the church. The procession was coming. The big doors opened at last. I had never seen choir boys wearing white surplices over scarlet gowns; they marched in pairs, slow and stately, their mouths opening and closing in song. 'Oh come let us adore Him, Oh come let us adore Him . . .'

'Watch this now, Ula. Look.' Maggie pushed me forward. Here came the priest at last. Maggie crossed herself, the Da bent his head. The Ma nudged me. Could I see?

'Which one is the priest, Maggie?'

The Ma rolled her little eyes. Disgraceful. Imagine not knowing a priest from a prayerbook, what a miserable heathen child. The incense bearer swung the censer. Thick white clouds scented the air. There was the priest, gold robes glittering, more singing, more incense, bright lights. Acolytes were bearing tall candles, the priest was nearing us now. I pushed my face through the railings. The new baby was on its way.

I had expected something exquisite, a pretty-faced porcelain doll in linen and lacy frills. The priest was carrying a lump of wood in a blanket, with a roughly-hewn blob of a face. It had two dabs for eyes and a smudged mouth. There wasn't any nose. It was even less complete-looking than Mary and Joseph; they deserved better than that in their hay. I looked round; no one else seemed to think it was curious, all the people's faces looked proud. Faces were smiling, they were singing. Now we could all go inside.

'You've seen it now, Ula. What did you think of it?' Maggie's face shone with delight. Christmas day had started now, we could hear mass next. I sat between her and Ma. She seemed to have completely forgotten her promise to Mamma about religion. You must hear mass at Christmas or risk your immortal soul. I didn't understand the Latin praying, I didn't understand what the priest did. Soon everyone left their seats to go to the altar to have something put in their mouths. They came back swallowing a little, with ecstasy in their eyes.

The street was even more full of people afterwards. We

were joined by men who had been on the spree. It was much colder now but no one noticed it, there was a special friendliness in the air. The four of us walked in a line. Maggie had a new hair slide on that her Da had given her, with six diamonds in a row that sparkled. We looked forward now to a cup of strong tea.

As Maggie and I got into bed in the back bedroom I heard the woman calling her cat again. I saw the hair slide with the diamonds on the pillow by me, I heard Maggie breathe and sigh. It was all so wonderful and exciting, I felt that nothing would be sad again.

I woke early and lay watching the line of chimneys beginning to show against the dark sky outside. My fingers felt still with cold outside the blankets but I could wait no longer, I must be first downstairs to look at the tree. Last night when we had come back from the church service it had shone out like a beacon of love. There might be presents there now, or sweets perhaps. What a pity I had nothing to give. Maggie didn't stir as I slipped from the bedclothes, she was snoring again on her back. The boards were icy, I could feel the nail heads, My dressing gown and slippers weren't unpacked. I found my coat on the nail on the door and my lace-up shoes and went slowly and carefully down.

The coloured lights showed intermittently in a line under the closed door. I opened it. Yes, there was the tree. It seemed to flash even more brightly in the light of dawn than it had last night. The paper chains were more colourful, the blue and yellow bird more alive. The cotton wool blobs bobbed in the windowframe. There was something long and bulky on the floorboards, something bigger than a sack. The lights flashed again, the sack moved by the bucket of stones. It sat up. It was a man in a blanket, not a sack or a present at all, just an ordinary man, watching me with horrid eyes.

'Hullo there. Are you looking for Santa Claus?'

'There is no Santa Claus. Only babies think there is. Who are you?'

'Who am I? Who am *I*? That's excellent, that is. Who are *you* I'd like to know?'

'I'm Ula.'

'Ula is it? And I'm Joe.'

'What are you doing? What do you want here?'

'I'm asked what I'm doing in my own home. That's excellent, that is. If it's any business of yours, which it is not, I've come back home for the Christmas. With a gift for my sister Margaret, I've a present for Maggie May.'

'You're not her brother, you can't be. Maggie is an only child.'

'Is that a fact now? Let me tell you then, I'm her brother, I live here. I've a present for her.'

'I don't believe you.'

'Turned out of my room, I was, by you and my sister, turned out like a dog in the road. You none of you gave a thought for me, did you? Pushed out like a dog I was.'

'I thought . . .'

'You thought? You'd best be thinking again. I slept here on the floor, but I'm back now, I'll have my bed back again.'

By the zinc bucket with the tree roots and stones was a newspaper packet. He picked it up.

'Here. Catch. Maggie's gift.'

It was bloody, red, dripping. Red dripped from his fingers and hand. Dark spots fell on the floor.

EIGHT

I don't remember leaving the house again that morning, or running down Maggie's street. I must have run a long time but I don't remember crossing the road. I don't remember seeing any windows with Christmas trees, or passing the church with the crib. I found myself under a streetlamp in a wide and empty street. My knees ached, my feet hurt, I was cold.

I had gone downstairs so eagerly to the waiting Christmas tree, longing to start the day. There was the capon to roast, the front room to make ready, the card table to deck with lace. Maggie had shown me the cloth they kept for special occasions with drawn threadwork round the edges, bleached as white as the choirboys' robes. I looked forward to arranging the red apples left over from Maggie's apple cake in a cracked white china bowl. The card table was to be my responsibility, I would place the cleaned cutlery just so.

Maggie had been up late last night, plucking the bird. She had let me stay up too. The Ma watched the wireless while Da smoked and had more to drink. The scullery floor had soon become white with the bird's feathers. The Da picked one up and started tickling me with it. He

79

whispered something and I'd squirmed. I hadn't minded although his eyes had gone silly, but Maggie got angry with him. She had told him not to be crude and the look in her eyes made me uncomfortable. She told me to gather up the feathers on the scullery floor into a newspaper. They were soft and fluffy and I loved them. The capon looked smaller now, its flesh was pink and sticky-looking, with pimples where the feathers had been. What did 'crude' mean? I took a feather to taste, lovely, a soft wet squashy feel. Maggie told me not to be dirty. It was nice that Nurse had gone from my life. Helping was lovely here, I'd never been up so late. The onions were chopped, the bread crumbled for the stuffing, the apple cake had been baked. I carried out all the rubbish to the yard for her. I listened again for the sad voice calling Tibby. The last job before going upstairs was to help clean the draining board to get rid of the onion smell. Maggie poured boiling water from the kettle while I scrubbed with washing soda and a brush. All the water had to be heated on the cooker; the scullery had filled with steam. In the morning we planned to put up the star, a big one made from silver paper. We'd discussed it as we'd undressed. We had closed the window after taking the clock away in case the snow came and blew on our bed. I watched her diamonds wink in the dark as she had prayed on her beads under the blanket. She had touched my forehead, saying she was blessing me and bother her promise to my mamma. My soul was more important than any promise. I'd been to mass, holy God, and the saints would be pleased.

As I had left the back bedroom in my coat and nightdress I'd heard snores from the Ma and Da. I don't know what presents I had hoped for. I knew that the family was poor. I wasn't used to getting presents. Perhaps I expected jewels, perfumes and flowers. I didn't imagine playthings. Tin was my only toy.

The sight of Maggie's brother had been a shock to me. He

wore old plimsoles and dirty dungarees. He reminded me of a snake in a blanket, he had unblinking horrid eyes. The tips of his teeth showed when he spoke to me. His voice hissed and he wriggled his shoulders very slightly. He had the same flap of hair as the Da, the same protuberant ears.

Maggie had woken then; she missed me in the bed with her. She came down with her face lumpy from sleep. Before she could say anything I accused her.

'Maggie, you never said anything about this brother person. He's been sleeping under the tree.'

'Under the tree is right,' he echoed. And he was her brother, right? Why had she not seen fit to mention him? He wasn't invisible or dead.

'Yes, why, Maggie? If he's your brother you should have told me. I thought you only had parents. Why?'

'It wouldn't be shame by any chance, Maggie. Could that be it? Eh?'

His hissing voice sank lower. It hadn't always been shame, had it? A different story once, eh, Maggie? His snake's eyes watched her closely. Thick as you like, one time, oh yes, just he and Maggie May. Now, when it suited her, she ignored him. Pushed into the cold like a dog. He'd been stretched on the floor all alone, on this cold Christmas night, on account of an English brat.

'I'm not a brat. I hope you aren't talking about me. I was invited. I didn't know you were alive.'

He went on looking at Maggie, he didn't look at me. He'd more right in this house than she had. *He'd* not run off to the other side, nor had he brought shame and scandal to the home. Nobody pointed the finger at him. Yet she had the audacity to come dancing back here for the Christmas, no apologies, no by your leave. Like a dog he'd been treated, and he wasn't having it; a dog without any home.

'Stop. Listen to me. Stop,' I shouted.

He turned. 'And listen, *you*. *You* stop, you're not needed here. Why don't you pack up and leave?'

Maggie begged us to be quiet. We'd wake the Ma and the Da, quietly now, for the love of the Sacred Heart. He hissed back again at her. She was a phoney and a sham. She'd done as she pleased from the very start, she'd no other concern than herself. Maggie started to cry loudly, her voice raising to a wail. Joe was a liar, and on Christmas morning. Joe was an evil star.

'You give me back my room, now, d'ye hear me? You and that brat. Out.'

Maggie clutched at her lollopers, she'd never done harm to Joe. She'd looked after the parents, she loved them, she'd always sent money home. Ma and Da needed her.

'It's true, Joe. I know it is.'

'Shut your gob, you. I didn't ask for your interference. As for you, Maggie, they need you back like they need poison. Did they ask you back? No.'

She'd always been a good daughter, she said. She'd not caused any heartache like him. Always out on the drink, stopping away at nights. Backing horses, losing at cards. He'd been better never to have been born.

'You didn't think so little of me one time, did you? Eh Maggie?'

'Evil speaker. Muckpot. Vile.'

'Muck is cheap, Maggie. Anyone can call names. Who made Ma strange in her ways? Who made her nerveses bad?'

'You done nothing for this family, Joe Mullen. What did you bring home today?'

He drew his chin in line with his neck, like a snake getting ready to strike. What had he brung? He'd brung this then. A Christmas gift. Here then, catch it and happy days.

Maggie screamed again as the liver parcel hit her and went slithering down her front. She was bloodied, her lollopers were stained with it. He was a Judas. A Christmas curse.

There were footsteps overhead. The Da came downstairs

first, his spikey hair showing patches of scalp. He wore his long underwear and stood looking at us. He seemed surprised to see Joe.

'So you decided to honour us after all, did you? What happened this time , Joe?'

He saw the blood staining Maggie's nightdress, he saw the mess on the floor. What was it? Liver? Jesus God, Joe, what is that?

Then Ma came in, smiling vaguely, looking like a bolster in her tight nightdress. She was confused, not really upset, her wireless was her soother of pain and her Joe was ever wild. The tree lights flashed again and she saw the blood. Holy saints. Holy saints. . . .

'The English brat is after having a nosebleed,' Joe said in a jeering tone. She saw the newspaper in another flash. She fumbled her short fat hands. There was no music at this time of the morning, she couldn't manage without Henry Hall. What was the shouting about? What was that newspaper? Holy saints . . . Nosebleed? Why should Maggie call Joe such names?

He was still kneeling, half in the blanket. He fiddled for his cigarettes, the carton was empty, he found a butt behind his ear. He struck a match on his thumb nail, blowing smoke out like poisonous gas. I hoped we might soon all be friends again. The Da went to get his pipe from the scullery.

'Here you are, Ma, don't say I didn't think of you.' Joe threw a small packet over to the Ma. It was a small white clay pipe. Her eyes looked less anxious. She put the pipe unlit in her mouth. I was glad that someone else was claiming her attention. I hadn't liked her commenting on my looks and grasping my chin.

'Shall I get some newspaper, Maggie, and put all this outside?'

'Leave it,' Joe shouted at me. He had a few things first to make clear. Ma and Da had better listen to him, and I had better listen too. He was still the son and heir of the household, Maggie or no Maggie, he wanted to make it quite plain. He'd come in late, he'd been busy lately, he'd not seen much of them, he'd allow. But now he was back, he was home for the Christmas, alive and kicking, no harm done. He had not expected to find his bed full of people, nor the place full of English trash. He wasn't having a strange English brat usurping him, pushing him out of his home like a dog.

'Wait now, son, you've been gone a long time. Maggie . . .'

'Maggie? That one, there's a few things you should know about her. She's nothing but a fraud and a . . .'

'Liar. Muckpot. Lies.'

The Da let out a roar. What was happening? What exactly did Joe mean? He shook his hair back from his ears. Go on then, Joe, explain. His daughter Maggie hadn't an impure or dishonest thought in her.

'That's good, that's excellent, so it is. Sister Maggie wasn't pure, since a child. You ask her about those games.'

'Lies, Liar. Lies.'

'Go on. Ask her.'

And who had started it then, yelled Maggie. Who had thought of the idea? The feathers, the tickling, the buttons. Judas. Muckpot and lies.

'Holy saints, Maggie, what's this you're saying? Aaagh.'

The little pipe dropped out of the Ma's mouth onto the floor, the tree lights wavered with a fizzing sound. Maggie's voice dropped, she sounded hoarse now. 'Twas Joe done the buttons, she'd never wanted to. She'd never liked the feathers touching, it was Joe.

'What's this about feathers?' the Ma asked vaguely.

'In her knickerses, of course. Maggie couldn't get enough.'

Ma said nothing, she went to the scullery. We heard the click of her wireless, but no sound. The tree lights crackled again, went black and stayed black.

'Jesus. 'Tis a fuse.'

From the scullery came the sound of Ma singing in a breathy voice. 'Oh come let us adore him, Christ the Lord.'

'That's excellent, that is. See what the sight of you done to her, Maggie. You made her nerveses go.'

'Now, Joe, don't talk so to your sister. Maggie never . . .'

'Shut your mouth, you old gobshite. Go back and deliver logs.'

'Mag-gie. Mag-gie. I want to go to the . . .'

Something wet hit my cheek, something slippery slid down my neck. Joe was throwing his liver about now. He must have gone out of his mind. It must have been then that I ran outside, away from the house with the tree.

I stood under the streetlamp with my breath wheezing and my hair sticking to my wet face. I would never go back there, I couldn't. It was a house of cruelty and fear. They threw raw meat at each other and called each other names. They didn't want me. What did gobshite mean? There was blood round my collar, my tears tasted dirty. I had no hanky for my streaming nose.

This street wasn't like Maggie's street, no church here, no crib or star. These houses had windows with curtains and front doors at the end of flagged paths. There were railings or low brick walls on either side of latched gates that protected flowerbeds or small patches of lawn. The door nearest the streetlamp had a holly wreath with red bows and 'Welcome' written inside it in careful silvery script. There must be children inside. Were they sleeping upstairs, dreaming of glittering gifts and trees? Would they dance round later in silk pleating and bows, pulling crackers and inventing games. Would they eat jelly and ice cream, showing bright teeth when they laughed? I had my nightdress on, I was aching and bloody, I wanted to go to the . . . I gripped the iron gate and cried.

I heard the door with the welcome sign open. Someone was coming down the path.

'Don't touch me. Leave me. *Leave* me.'

A large hand was on my shoulder. 'It's Ula, isn't it? From the dancing class? You won't remember me. I'm Lucy's father. Come on. Lucy is inside.'

NINE

My life changed when I saw her again. She wasn't in bed dreaming about presents but sitting at her own kitchen table and watching me. She looked just the same. Of course, Lucy was Irish and this nice house must be her home. I had only seen her once at Miss Dance's class, wearing her bright silk pleated dress. Here she was at home in Ireland looking at me. She didn't have her monkey now.

'Oh there you are, Lucy. Is this your house?'

Her father had brought me inside without questioning me. Lucy wore her dressing gown now, of the same pink as her dancing dress, trimmed with shamrocks round the sleeves. She didn't look surprised.

'You do look awful. You've got marks all over your neck and face. You've been crying.'

Her kitchen was light and warm with two sinks and draining boards behind her at the far end. I had stopped crying but my breath caught as I breathed. The father took me to the hot tap and wiped me with a warm damp cloth. Then he dried me with large firm hands without speaking.

'You look awful,' Lucy said again.

The house was used as a guesthouse for students which he and Lucy ran alone. The kitchen floorboards were a smooth salmon pink shade to tone with the curtains and walls. Their range had a grate in it where coal was burning. A lovely smell came from the oven. They'd put a turkey in early to cook slowly; the smell was the stuffing she'd made.

She didn't question me, nor did her father; they accepted me just as I was, without clothes, filthy and tear-stained, not knowing from where I had run. She said that it was a good thing I'd got here early; their students had all gone to their own homes for the holiday. Their bird was too big for the two of them, I could help them eat it. They were setting off themselves after dinner for the country where her grandmother lived. They often went in the holidays and always at Christmas time.

Their refrigerator and store cupboards seemed to be packed with foods that I'd never seen. Crystallized fruits in wooden boxes, caviar in interesting jars, ginger in blue-painted vases, dates packed in rows with a tiny serving fork. Mock beams across the ceiling had hooks where vegetables were strung. I had never seen onions plaited, nor known about garlic roots. But apart from the turkey in the oven Lucy said it was all ordinary food. She and her father believed in keeping a good table. Did I feel like a malted milk? I said I'd never tried it. I watched the neat way she poured and heated the milk in a copper-bottomed saucepan before stirring the powder in. We drank it from pink and gold cups and saucers that had pictures of the little English princesses wearing coral beads and frilled frocks. Lucy's aunt in England had sent them she told me with distaste, she was antiroyalist herself. I looked at their curls and their faces while I sipped the sweet-tasting drink. Lucy said that her grandmother had taught her to cook. It was something she took very seriously, she had to learn all she could early because she wanted to become a chef. She'd never had any other ambition since she'd heard the Three Bears story as a baby. She'd have been ashamed to serve porridge that wasn't right. Her stuffing was a secret recipe that she'd invented herself and that she'd take with her to the grave. I remembered Maggie's humble stuffing. Lucy was a being apart. I pleated the edge of the pink linen tablecloth. I wanted to talk to her about what had happened, but not now. She showed no curiosity, repeating that I looked awful. Now that I was hearing her speak I thought she had a pretty voice with a chuckle in it. She had the faintest trace of an accent, nothing broad like Maggie had. She said that she and her father didn't keep Christmas in the usual way, they just had a festive dinner. The rest of it was too much bother and fuss. They disliked trees and decorations, they didn't exchange any gifts. She spoke with condescension about the frenzy and waste of time. She'd outgrown it all long ago. Presents and balloons were all right for babies; if she wanted something her father got it for her.

'Don't you go to church then, Lucy? I thought Irish people did.'

She stared, she smiled with scorn. She pleased herself, so did her father, she wasn't made to go when she was at home. She believed in making up her own mind when she wasn't at her convent school. Saint Lucy was patron of the blind, her name saint, there was more than one way of being blind. Religion was for easily lead people who preferred to avoid the truth. She turned her back on that rigmarole. Most people were like sheep. Her grandmother was a believer, but she was elderly. Lucy aimed to become a cordon bleu chef. One day people would come to her to learn gourmet dishes. And besides, her grandmother had a financial interest in Christmas: the forestry commission farmed a part of her land. Christmas trees grew in abundance behind Grandma's manor. Lucy disliked them herself. Grandma had given Lucy a set of chef's knives recently, in a polished box all graded to size. Over there on the dresser, would I like to see them? I didn't like any sort of knife. She had a chef's cap and apron, she put on the cap to show me. Her wedgwood-blue eyes were bright.

'It does suit you, Lucy,' I said admiringly.

It would be her uniform one day, when she was free of her convent school. She'd lead her cordon bleu institution before becoming a master chef. She'd work in the best kitchens of the biggest hotels.

'I don't go to school yet. Only Miss Dance's class. My sisters are going to boarding school soon. I'm not very fond of knives. Can I see your school uniform?'

She pulled a face at the memory of Miss Dance. She remembered me there all right. Had I still got that giraffe?

'Yes. Have you got your black monkey?'

She had no time now for stuffed animals, she'd left him behind with Miss Dance. I thought she was very grown-up. I agreed earnestly when she said dolls were boring and that vocations mattered most. She only ever read recipe books. What books did I like best? I was ashamed to tell her that I couldn't properly read. I said I liked books about films.

Lucy had a lot of stuffed animals left over from her younger days, all named after hotels. There was Gresham, Hibernia, Shelbourne; her monkey had been called Wicklow. We'd go up and look at them soon. I had forgotten that I was still in my nightdress. My feet felt warm again now. Her father had left us alone with our Horlicks. He was kind. I was all right here. When he asked me where I'd been staying I was confused again. It couldn't be far away if I was there this morning, Lucy said sharply. Surely I knew where. Fancy coming all the way from England and not finding that out. What a baby, worse than a newborn lamb.

'She's three years younger than you, Lucy. She's had an upsetting time.'

Her father would telephone my mother in England. Meanwhile I was not to fret. He was delighted to have me here, I could stay. His Lucy needed a friend. We heard him speaking in the breakfast room through the hatchway, where the telephone was. What would Mamma say to him? I tried to imagine her, alone now, with her face perhaps petulant from sleep. Had her peace been disturbed again? Had she no escape from a child even from across the sea? Was she happy? Was she in her dressing gown? It was Christmas. Would she marry someone else?

'Ula,' he called to me. My mother wanted to speak to me.

'I don't want to. I can't . . .'

'Just say hallo. To let her know you're . . . just hallo.'

'Hallo? Mamma? Hallo?'

So far away, such a tinny sound. Could that voice be Mamma? I wasn't used to the telephone. At home I whispered into it without asking for a number. I was expected to talk now and listen.

'Darling child, what has happened? You're not unhappy, are you? You don't want to come back? Why?'

'Mamma? Mamma?'

'After all my instructions to Cookie, what was she thinking about? Imagine letting you out alone so early. I hope she's not making you pray. . . .'

'Mamma? . . .'

He took the receiver from my hand, dampened from where I'd clenched. What a good thing she couldn't see me, all tear-stained, with liver blood down my coat. Lucy was grinning again.

'You do look awful.'

We listened while he spoke again. 'Unhappy'. . . 'troubled house' . . . 'lost her way'. He slid the hatch across but we could still hear him. He was talking about the visit to his own mother later in the day. I held my breath. When he came back to us in the kitchen he said that my mother had agreed. I could stay on here, I could go with them to the country. I'd be most welcome at Lucy's grandmother's home. She had a big house further north.

A country estate sounded grand. Perhaps the grandmother had a title. It was to be a manor in the country for me instead of Cookie in the slums. Finding Lucy was a turning point; I knew I'd have peace of mind, though my head still felt thick and giddy and my eyes hurt. It was natural and peaceful here with wonderful Lucy, an anti-Catholic, an antiroyalist, a cordon bleu chef-to-be. The father said he'd let his mother know at once to expect me. She'd be charmed. He had found out Maggie's address from my mother, no question of my going back there. He'd go round now and pick up my things. My mother had given her authority. We would eat our dinner and leave for the country. We must leave in good time because snow was forecast.

I sighed and waved my toes. Lucy and I were alone.

We went upstairs to her bedroom to look in her fitted cupboards all along one wall. There was her pink frock with the silk pleating that I'd remembered. There were her red dancing shoes. Her convent uniform was maroon with a Latin motto on the blazer pocket which meant 'God is love'. She hated her nuns and their teachings. They made you have a bath under a sheet. The food was awful and they slapped you. She occupied her time in the chapel services by inventing recipes and making secret plans. She wouldn't remain long in a hotel kitchen, she would work in a palace one day.

'Which palace, Lucy?'

A large one, she said, but not in England, of that I could be very sure. She hummed and looked at her hair in the mirror, beautiful, calm, sure. She said there was her cot of stuffed animals, each with the hotel name. If I wanted I could put my giraffe in with them later. I knew he'd be better alone with me; his sucked hooves and flaking tin spots would be sorry and out of place amongst all that furred opulence. Lucy believed that childhood was far from pleasurable, it was a time to be lived quickly until you were free. She had already invented a celebration cocktail for when she started periods. I didn't ask what she meant. I wanted to agree with her over everything. Only yesterday I had longed for Bruno's bottle and to be wrapped in woollen shawls. Meeting Lucy had changed my course. She inspired me. I too would stamp in high heels before drinking whiskey and blinking at men. She said that I had a lot to learn about life; those servants in England had me spoiled.

'Has your grandmother got servants?'

I imagined a manor house would be staffed with butlers. Only cleaning women, Lucy said. Not that her grandmother wasn't prosperous; more importantly she was quite a good cook. The manor was a remote place in large grounds. Only Lucy was allowed in the kitchen besides grandmother.

'Oh, Lucy, I love your bedroom.'

More salmon-coloured curtains were at her windows, but with a tiny blue sprigged pattern matching her bed spread and frilled dressing table. Her ceiling was a silvery blue, her bathroom opening from the bedroom was blue, as blue as her lovely blue eyes. It seemed that she already did live in a palace. She and her father had taken me in knowing nothing about my worries. Did she know that my brother had died? Had she noticed my white hair? Soon I would be in a country estate. They had a lake with swans on it. Foxes and deer lived in their woods, coming up near the house in bad weather. I hoped to see the deer stepping daintily over the lawn or a fox sniffing round the bins at the back. Long ago there had been peacocks on the lawns to parade amongst the flowerbeds, and gardeners were employed. The family fell on hard times and the estate declined, the peacocks disappeared. They were stupid and small-minded birds, Lucy said; where one went the others followed. Legend had it that they were broken-hearted, they were beautiful but without brain. God punished their vanity by giving them an ugly shriek but no song. There was said to be a ghost peacock at the manor but Lucy hadn't seen it, nor did she believe in ghosts. She disliked legend and lore as much as she disliked religion and royalty.

'Are the lawns there green as a parable?'

She told me not to talk rubbish. We would go down now and get on with preparing the meal. Her clothes were already packed for the country. When her father got back again I didn't ask what he had thought of Maggie's family or if she had asked about me. I was ashamed of her. I wanted to forget all of them as well as the tree, the church with the crib in that street. They hated each other, they weren't loving and affectionate. I didn't understand them; I didn't want to.

Lucy said that we'd eat in the kitchen, we'd be informal and save time. She moved lightly from the stove to the table. She let me put out the mats. Although it was the kitchen it seemed formal and festive. The refrigerator lit up when you opened it, showing all the beautiful coloured foods. I was glad not to eat near the telephone in case Mamma wanted to speak to me again. Lucy and her father sat at opposite ends of the table, I with my back to the range. I was dressed properly again in my skirt and jersey. Lucy wore pastel blue. We ate mashed potatoes whipped with sour cream and herbs. The small green sprouts were lightly steamed. I had never tasted such rich gravy. Lucy's cooking was best of all.

'Oh, Lucy, your cooking is wonderful.'

I wanted her to be glad that I'd come there. I said I could understand why cooking was her life's work. Her father dismembered the turkey carefully, laying portions onto an oval plate for their student guests when they returned. The cuisine was the pride of the guest house. The refrigerator was never bare. We ate cheeses and fruit after the turkey, before our coffee and turkish delight. Lucy was contemptuous of mince pies and puddings, the popular fare for mindless sheep people. I had never eaten a slice of melon served with ginger or seen turkish delight in an icing-sugar cloud. My piece tasted like Mamma's rose water with nuts in it. I listened to Lucy's pretty voice. Her dream world would become mine. I too would become polished and sophisticated. I too would choose a career. Her father asked what plans I had, what I would do when I grew up. I faltered. A mother, I supposed . . . to become married.

'Is that all?' Lucy said loftily. Her father was talking about a vocational future. I hadn't decided, I might be a vet I said. For rare animals naturally, nothing ordinary. My name meant 'bird' actually, I added in an offhand way. Lucy said I should study ornithology, if I wasn't too bird-brained to work. Outside their kitchen was a paved yard with urns for plants to grow in. There was a bird table and a stone birdbath. Go out now and put scraps for them, Lucy ordered. I was proud to feed their birds. There was a bag of nuts for the blue tits. I looked at a sparrow pecking at a bread crust and thought of the ghost peacock bewailing its pea-sized brain. Mamma had a gauze dress in peacock colours, multicoloured, iridescent, divine.

I sat in the back of the car with Lucy for the long drive to the manor house. Her father tucked a rug lined with fur over us; coney fur Lucy told me, a posh name for rabbit skin. I stroked it slowly. That little scrap of fluff from her dress at the dancing class had brought her to me after all. I asked her what the tune she kept humming was called. She smiled and didn't reply. Did she know a tune about Come adore Him? She pulled a face. Don't ask her to think of hymns, she wasn't at the convent now. She told her father to drive faster, she had a lot to tell Grandma tonight. She was like a princess in fur, giving orders. I'd see the green countryside soon, the delight of Maggie's heart. The county we were visiting was agricultural, with many lakes to make everything lush.

'Maggie's mother came from there, I think it was there.' I felt bolder about mentioning them now. I wondered if they were still shouting. Was the Ma watching her wireless still?

It felt nice to have Tin with me again. Because of my tired feet I wore my bedroom slippers for travelling, their brown pompoms soft as two old friends. I would need wellingtons for the country, they told me. The walking was wet and rough. My eyes felt heavy but I didn't want to miss the scenery and the sight of the yellowish sky. It would snow tonight, the father said. It was weather to keep folk at home. Not that he minded. It meant that we'd have a clear run.

We drove through the small towns of Ireland. Some were just a single street. They all had pubs and churches. The houses opened onto the pavements like the houses in Maggie's street. The doorsteps were cleanly whitened in honour of the day, though there were few Christmas trees in the windows. I saw no decorations or coloured lights. A few general stores selling everything had greetings cards on display. A bearded Santa Claus made of cardboard had a sack of net Christmas stockings containing holly sprigs and cheap tin toys. Nothing looked exotic, precious or rare here. The Irish country seemed bleaker somehow. A live kitten was curled on a white baby shawl, the sign said 'For Babies' needs'. A window was devoted to first communion clothing with little plaster models wearing white. They held rosaries in their stiff plaster fingers, their mouths simpered under cheap cotton veils anchored with wax orange blossom wreaths. Lucy made a 'yuk' sound in her throat. On a bare stretch of road I saw a wayside shrine with lone statue holding shrivelled flowers. I turned back to see the face, watching travellers, pale and cold, wondering which saint it was. Lucy showed no interest; such effigies were for sheep. There were no other cars for miles.

They always stopped at Cootehill; it had become a ritual. They went to the hotel to let the grandmother know they were almost there. Grandmother was particular about punctuality. She must not be upset, being elderly. Lucy's father was her only son and Lucy her only grandchild. How lucky she was not to have to compete for attention and to have a country and a town home.

While her father went to the telephone she and I went to

the lounge. Her voice was loud and assured as she ordered
malted milks before sitting on a red plush chair. I sat opposite her, hoping my bedroom slippers weren't absurd. I
pulled my coat over my legs. I'd never been in a hotel. Lucy
drummed her long fingers on the table top. She'd asked for
a whiskey for her father as well. What confidence you have,
Lucy, how I admire your verve. The milk drink, when it
came, tasted different from her brew, more like honey and
much too sweet. I gazed at her while she sipped disdain-
fully. She was twice as nice as my sisters and her father was
wonderful too. He drank his whiskey quickly like Maggie's
men had, but without their runny eyes and watery smiles. I
watched the way his fingers held the glass, loosely, with
splayed tips and very short nails. He leaned forward over
his knees a little, but keeping his back straight. I liked his
brogues and his ribbed socks. Lucy, how lucky you are.
Outside the street was deserted, inside the hotel seemed
full. The lights shone white and glaring in the bar next to
us. I watched a woman there, speaking with a loud voice.
She leaned across to kiss the bartender, showing full
breasts under her blouse. She whispered, fluttering her
eyelids yearningly, her blouse neck slipped some more.
Was this the world my mother wanted, lipstick, admiration
and men? It's dangerous to have too much feeling. Don't
feel guilty, don't involve yourself, self comes first.

Lucy showed me the cloakroom. She had to go often like
me. It made a bond between us, I thought happily, as we
walked along the passageway. Her shadow towered above
mine as she waved her arms, pulling a face. 'Look out, here
comes a ghostie.' I kicked my slippers. 'You are funny,
Lucy. I do like you.' She could still touch her nose with her
tongue.

We washed under the same jet of hot water after soaping
lavishly with pink hotel soap. We licked the lather from our
hands, we smeared it, we rubbed until our lips were sore. I
asked if she liked Jeyes fluid, or the smell of syrup of figs.

She liked soap flakes and scouring powder she told me, and that pink powder for cleaning knives. Don't forget her heart lay in the kitchen. That was enough of playing baby games, dry my mouth and follow her.

Before we left the cloakroom we polished the surrounds with folded towels. We breathed on the brass taps before buffing them. We folded the towels corner to corner. We arranged the toilet rolls to hang exactly. We rubbed the door handles and locks on the lavatories, breathing with concentration and care. We peered into a cleaning cupboard and found a vast vacuum cleaner surrounded with snakelike coils. Lucy patted her hair complacently. Could I really not even boil an egg? The steam from our labours had turned to little diamonds in the fuzz round her temples. She wondered if the white parts in my hair made me an albino. You got freaks in animals too. She'd seen an albino blackbird once. Still, I'd made a good job of the taps.

'The last lap of the journey,' the father said, tucking the rabbit rug round us again. I loved the feel of it on my knees as much as I loved him caring for me. Lucy pointed at my hair again, had he noticed? He said it was distinguished and that I'd be glad of it one day. I shouldn't allow anyone to scoff. I was a pretty child and I'd be prettier when I was older. I knew he meant that Lucy was the best.

He told me to look out on the left side of the car; I mustn't miss the first glimpse of their lake. It was said to bring luck when you saw it, provided you didn't speak first. Many Irish lakes had legends attached to them; they were especially proud of theirs. It wasn't large but was interestingly shaped, with a dense growth of woodland around.

It was almost dark when we turned into the big gates and along a twisting lane. Humped shapes of rhododendrons grew on either side of us, their stiff leaves tapped at the car. In summertime the blooms made a fine sight, mauvey reds, orange and pink. Now you couldn't see any colour in the failed light. The tall conifers stretched upwards behind the bushes darkly filling the sky.

'There now, Ula, that's the lake, see?'

'Where? That? Where are the swans?'

A break in the trees and rhododendrons showed a stretch of what looked like mud. As the moon came from behind a cloud it glistened weakly. It was hard to tell what was mud and what was water. The land round the tip of the lake was marshy, the father said, and the only point where the water could be reached, the woods elsewhere being thick and impenetrable. The lake was actually heart-shaped, a heart with a twisted tip. We stopped and watched. Then the moon hid itself and we drove away, turning another bend. I asked again about the swans. They nested in the reeds and sedges, being shy and retiring birds. The old wood was a reserve for wild life now, since his mother had been in charge. It was the birds' and animals' sanctuary, and had become their sole domain.

'I can go in,' Lucy said boastfully.

'No. You know the rule.'

The new wood behind the manor was cultivated for Christmas trees. It was a source of income for the grand-mother and gave work for local men. I would see every-thing in the morning. Lucy started humming her tune again. We were nearing her second home.

We drew up before a big house with a pointed gable and its windows blazing with light. In the pillared porch stood the grandmother waiting with stretched arms to us. She was taller than Lucy's father, with white hair and a clinging shawl.

TEN

'So Lucy my childie, you and Ula shall go early to gather green for the party.'

'Not a Christmas tree, Grandma, you surely don't mean a tree?'

The grandmother laughed. Indeed no, we'd all had enough of trees. Weren't there enough outside the house to fill the universe? Her voice had the same chuckle as Lucy's had. I was awed by her stately height. She was relying on our help for tomorrow's party, the one she held every year. She always asked the same guests to it, quiet people without many human ties. They relied on the grandmother's St Stephen's Day tea party as a part of their yearly feast. The big hall was decked with greenery, the long refectory table was loaded with food. Games followed later, with hot punch round the fire at the end.

Lucy and I must gather as much greenery as we could carry. There was plenty growing on the edge of the old wood. Bring in all the holly and ivy we could find. Grandmother was delighted that I'd joined them, she could well use another pair of hands. Just take from the edge of the wood, not inside it.

'I hope I see that ghost peacock. Who is that man in the

picture?'

'There isn't a peacock, I told you,' said Lucy. No one had seen it, it was rot. The man in the picture was her grandfather, his face peered from a heavy frame. Because he was dead a lamp burned there. It was the first thing you saw when you got inside. The great hall had big fireplaces each end of it where wood and turf burned high. The mantelpieces were marble under carved gold mirrors. The grandfather's picture was like a shrine. When he'd been alive much of the country round had belonged to the manor but all was sold now except for the two woods. Grandmother stared at me piercingly. Had Lucy explained about her animal sanctuary, the woods where no one must go? I could run as much as I wished in the new woods and admire the plantation, but not into the old woods at all. Come now to the fire and talk a little. I had had a tiring day. She wanted to explain about the tasks ahead of us, the most important being the greenery. There was last-minute baking, scones and jam sponges, and setting out the table with the best china. Had I a suitable frock for her party? She didn't mention my hair. She questioned us about church-going, her voice and eyes quite severe.

'Daddy and I went to midnight mass, Grandma,' Lucy said quickly. And I knew she was afraid of her. You did what the grandmother wished or lied about it. You kept busy, you practised the faith. She expected you to rise early, not to be idle and to keep a cheerful face. She said that if we were warmed through we should go up now to our bedrooms.

'Can we share, Grandma?'

'Share, Lucy? I beg your pardon, what do you mean?'

'Ula might be lonely. She's not used to sleeping alone, she might get frightened.'

I felt my cheeks go warm with pleasure. It must mean that Lucy wanted me. Or was she just belittling me? The grandmother's reply was terse. No question of sharing at the manor, Lucy ought to know that. The rooms must be silent upstairs, bedrooms were for sleeping and praying, not chattering, especially at night.

She walked up the wide stairway with the polished treads and banisters that lead upwards to the gallery. Her strap shoes made little taps. Lucy was behind her, I came next, the father followed with our bags. I looked back over the banisters at the grandfather's picture, following us with his eyes. I felt the heat rising from the two burning turf fires. The grandfather's eyes seemed to burn as well. The stairs curved round to join the gallery. The grandmother moved like Lucy, her back straight, her small feet pointing slightly out. She turned. She would put me in the room next to Lucy's. Lucy always slept in the room on her own. It was quite unnecessary for me to feel strange here, Lucy and she would be near. The father would sleep at the end. The rooms facing the back of the house overlooking the new wood were kept closed in winter, the cost of heating was high.

My room was beautiful. It was large, sparsely furnished and warm. Instead of curtains shutters were in the windows, another fire burned in the grate. The grandmother crossed to bolt the shutters, they were the best thing for keeping out draughts. Before I slept, she warned me, I must open them; fresh air was important at night. The age and size of the house made heating difficult, they only used turf and logs. I was responsible for the fire in my bedroom, I must take care to use fuel with care. She bent to put another sod on it. The ash was an orangey shade. The bed near the fireplace was ready for me, the sheets and blankets turned down over the eiderdown. Tidiness was a virtue, the grandmother said quietly; the care and condition of my room depended on me. I looked at the dark grey eiderdown that matched the carpeting. I looked at the white satin striped walls. There was an antique dressing table and wardrobe and a small grey armchair by the bed. Looking after this room would be a pleasure; I already felt proud and calm. Over the bed hung a crucifix inlaid with mother of pearl. Everything was tended and appreciated; there was nothing cheap, flashy or worn.

'I went to church last night with Maggie. I saw the holy child get born.'

The grandmother smiled indulgently. She was glad that I had a little faith in spite of my English ways. Faith was an anchor, it sustained you, faith kept you from straying from right. Lucy interrupted her. I wasn't Catholic, I didn't know anything about faith, didn't even go to school. I had no father, I didn't know a single prayer at all.

'I do. I do. I know "Hail".'

' "Hail"? Go on. Hail who?' sneered Lucy.

'That's enough, Lucy.' We were not to bicker, said grandmother, it was time now to go to bed. She would call me herself in the morning. And remember, I must make my bed. I could use the bathroom at the end of the gallery, but separately, not together with Lucy. Bath in the morning, not at night-time. The boiler didn't run to extra water at night. And no more talking now, children.

I had never seen or smelled turf burning, a delicate and romantic smell, like a bonfire only heavier. I lay in bed sniffing it, feeling rested. I watched the stuked sods sending sparks upwards; they glowed redly before sinking to ash. I was frightened of the grandmother, I'd make her like me. I would gather piles of holly and ivy and earn her praise. Before she left to go down again she had bent over me. Her cold closed lips just touched my head. Remember, child, fresh air, let the fire die out and, if I could manage it, say some kind of prayer. Any prayer was better than no prayer, the intention would be pleasing to God. If I wished I might call her Grandma. And now, Ula child, goodnight.

I put my hands over my face, I knelt by the bedside. 'Hail. All hail. Hello nonsense.' What were the prayers that

Maggie had said? Was that tapping from where the crucifix hung? Perhaps Lucy was trying to signal. I tried to knock back but my knuckles felt useless. More sparks flew up the chimney making patterns on the fireback. I was safe and comfortable here. Sleeping alone wasn't alarming, my bed was lovely, though my feet were still a little sore from the shoes. Tomorrow I might see deer on the lawns outside my window or the track of foxes' pads. Did the deer sleep standing up or lying? It had been a long Christmas day.

'It's six o' clock now, Ula. There's been a heavy fall of snow.'

'Does that mean we can't get the greenery?'

Grandma said the snow had stopped now, plans remained the same. As soon as Lucy and I had finished breakfast we must start on our first task outside. They could lend me a Burberry and wellingtons, my tweed coat and shoes wouldn't do.

Downstairs Lucy's father had already refilled the turf and log baskets, having raked and relaid various fires. Smoke was rising from the two fireplaces in the main hall; soon the flames would start to flare. The cleaning women who helped Grandma wouldn't be coming today, but Lucy was here and Lucy would be famous one day. Lucy made delicious fruit cakes, Grandma told me. And she'd find me some little jobs in the scullery. I would feel useful, I had no need to feel left out.

We sat at the refectory table for breakfast. Grandma said that monks had sat there once. They had used the same polished chairs that we were using, so mind now how we behaved. She didn't sit down herself but strode up and down with her porridge bowl in her hand. Each time she passed grandfather's picture she paused and looked at it. She never sat for breakfast, preferring to organize the day while she ate. She watched Lucy and me critically. Ula, don't hold your knife like a pen. Kitchen manners were difficult to break later; the result of giving servants too much power. My mamma would see the change in me when I returned to her, I would benefit greatly from my stay. As for herself she was delighted to have me, I'd be such a help with the chores.

Drifts of snow had pushed between the opened windows and the shutters during the night, little white walls of it. Lucy and I knocked them down with our hands. A larger wall of snow was inside the porch, up against the heavy front door. Grandma gave us two brooms. We must sweep the snow onto the path. There were shovels and a huge brush and pan. Outside I blinked, the glare was blinding. Maggie had been right after all, Irish snow was different, as different as Irish grass. It did look whiter, brighter, a blinding spiritual white.

'The sun makes the snow look like diamonds, Lucy.'

She banged the head of her broom down, giving me a pitying look. Next Grandma gave me a pail of peelings and tea leaves to carry out to the bins. The kitchen and back scullery overlooked the new wood with the plantation. There were the Christmas trees growing in rows, bordering aisles of untrodden bright snow. The trees looked paler, a delicate yellowish green, not tall yet but enough of them to stock the windows of the world. The air was still. I could hear nothing. I stood by the bins listening and watching. I didn't want to go in.

At breakfast Lucy had asked for brown sugar; Grandma had frowned and refused. Porridge was eaten with salt at the manor, Lucy ought to know that. She didn't encourage the development of a sweet tooth, particularly in a child. She herself used little sugar even in making cakes. I told her that I liked salt myself, and vinegar and mustard too. At home I used to help Maggie grate salt blocks. I crushed breadcrumbs and took rubbish to the bins. I had tidied too and cleaned saucepan lids, I liked being with Maggie best. Grandma had smiled coldly and approvingly. Quite the little maid of all work, wasn't I? I'd be most useful here. She repeated that she liked well-brushed teeth at the breakfast table as well as well-brushed hair. What was the red ribbon I was wearing? It didn't look very neat. I hadn't had time to tie it, I explained. It was from the tangerines that Maggie had bought. 'But you are not with Maggie now, child, are you? Do remember, sparkling teeth.'

'Hurry up out there, scullery maid,' Lucy called me. Time to gather greenery now. The father was stacking more logs. The snow on them hissed when he put them to burn, the turf smelled even stronger now. He asked Grandma if the usual assembly was coming. She nodded; her lonely ones who were dear to her. Would he organize the hot punch as usual? Her guests liked to warm up before they left. There was the vet who appreciated his toddy, and with whom she was on most friendly terms. They had common interests concerning animals, she in providing a sanctuary, he in curing their ills. The man with the travelling van came each year with his daughter; he supplied sundry items to the locality. Biscuits, shampoo sachets, boots and corn plasters were brought to remote cottage and farm dwellers. The van man's daughter helped take the change. The two spinster sisters from Cootehill did dressmaking for local people. They loved wild life too, especially birds. They stood in the porch each year with their backs to the big doorway, hoping to see a whooper swan or a long-eared owl while they waited for Grandma. The ban on entering the old wood was a disappointment. They would have enjoyed a walk there with notebooks and field glasses. The five guests knew and accepted each other's foibles. The sisters were brought by the van man, the vet came each year on his bike. Lucy's wellingtons had been bought from the van man; she showed me them in the cloakroom.

'These will fit. Put them on. Here.'

'They're too big for me, Lucy. Much too big.'

'Don't fuss. It's your feet are too small.'

She hoped that I wasn't going to complain all the while

and spoil everything. Here, take this mac, put it on. Her eyes had the hard blue colour of happiness as we started over the upper lawn on the snow. There were few red berries about this year, but she loved gathering holly branches best. I closed my lips over my teeth to stop the cold hurting them. Lucy went much too fast. My feet slipped in the boots, I couldn't keep up with her. The mac was too long as well. I squeezed my eyes up. I only needed to see Lucy, making a dark shape ahead in the snow. The holly trees were on the edge of the old wood, the ivy trailed over nearby shrubs. She had brought her biggest chef's knife for the branches, spurning Grandma's secateurs blunted from age. Inside Scots pine grew, larches, oak and silver birch. Seasonal evergreen only, Grandma said, just holly and ivy. There was plenty of this outside the wood. Lucy flashed her big knife importantly, she shook the branches, snow slithered down in little showers. She'd made me take her smallest knife before we came out, though I hated it. To please Grandma I'd gather a lot of green, both ivy and dark prickled holly leaves. She'd see then how clever and useful I was.

'Wait, Lucy, don't go so fast.'

'You're afraid, aren't you? You're a milksop.'

'I'm not afraid. I'm not a milksop. It's the boots, they're far too big.'

Her own boots fitted her trimly; she made accurate prints in the snow. As well as pointing them outwards like Grandma they had the same coloured eyes as well. She paused, staring upwards as the snow showered, she whistled that strange little tune. It looked like more snow falling when she shook the branches. In the dark shadows below were frosted drifts. Were there fox and rabbit holes under us? Did the squirrels nest over our heads? Snow fine as powder clouded the air again.

'My collar's wet Lucy, don't do that.'

She made a face. Scullery maid. I ought to be grateful

instead of complaining. If I couldn't keep up I shouldn't have come. She slashed at a higher branch. There was no room for milksops here.

'I'm not. I'm not.'

'You are. Inside, you know you are.'

We were just inside the old wood now. The trees grew closer. She was working systematically, flashing her knife back and forth. The holly branches were soon piling on the snow. Scullery maid. Milksop. Complainer. Why hadn't I stayed at home? She seized a hard chunk of snow.

'Don't, Lucy. It's cold. I'm your guest. Don't throw it.'

She hurled it, missing me. Guest? Don't imagine I was needed or wanted here. No one wanted a complainer. 'Scull-ery maid. Milk-sop. Complain-er.' More chunks flew through the air, then some twigs, then a stone. The stone grazed my cheek, it hurt, it could have blinded me. Had the old wood turned Lucy's brain? Where was the friend I'd longed for? Who was this stranger with snow and knives? She came closer, she waved her knife again. Poor milksop, did I want more?

'Stop. Stop, Lucy.'

'Why? I don't want you. Nor does Grandma.'

I felt the knife-tip touch my neck.

'I'll tell Grandma and your father if you don't stop.'

'No one will believe *you*.'

I felt the knife pressing.

'I'll do anything. I'll give you anything.'

'You haven't a thing that I want. Pauper. Milksop. All right then. I'll take that old tin giraffe.'

'But you can't. You don't like toys, you don't play with them.'

The knife pressed. 'I'll take the giraffe.'

I'd unpacked Tin and forgotten him since I'd been here. I was being paid now for neglect. She didn't want or need him, she'd no interest, she only wanted to wield her power. Her bears in the cot with hotel names meant nothing to her.

I couldn't bear to think of Tin thrown aside.

'Lucy, just because you have a father and two houses and a grandma . . .'

The knife pressed harder. It hurt. 'All right, you can have him . . . You can have him.'

She lowered the knife, smiling again. Right then, we still had a lot more to do. She wouldn't forget my promise. I watched her in silence as she cut down swatches of ivy. I had betrayed my toy. In a sharp tone she told me to gather it. I was a hindrance more than a help. Soon she had cut quite a pile. We took our raincoat belts off to bind the branch ends, ready to drag them back over the snow. I had cut no greenery. We didn't speak again until we'd reached the porch, pulling the branches behind.

'Remember, you promised. I'm having that toy of yours. Don't think I'll forget, I won't.'

I went back to my room quickly. There was poor Tin with my red ribbon round him, balanced in front of the fire. The room felt lovely again after the bitter air outside. I put more turf on the fire, doing it carefully. I watched more sparks fly. I didn't want to go to the party. It was safe here and smelled lovely in my room.

Grandma called and I had to go down. I hid Tin under my knickers in the big wardrobe. I brushed my hair to make it lie behind my shoulders. Should I try and walk like Lucy, with my toes out? I wished my eyes were a bit more blue.

Grandma was in the kitchen by the big range. Her apron was whiter than her hair. Lucy was measuring butter at the table. There was a smell of nutmeg, milk and dried fruit. Rows of fresh scones lay cooling on wire cake racks. There was a lump of dough waiting to be rolled and cut into circles.

'Will you make jam rock cakes too, Grandma?'

'Jam? In a rock cake? Fruit, Ula. A rock cake is made with fruit.'

She instructed me to flour the dough and then roll it.

Great heaven, not like that. Lucy must show me, knead it evenly, then take the round scone cutter and press.

Inside the house Lucy was quiet again, her eyes lost their malicious gleam. She was afraid of Grandma. Away from her she was different. I resolved to keep near Grandma's side. Lucy showed me how to push your palms forward, curling the fingers from the dough like a cat. My hands weren't as agile as hers were. I could feel she despised me when we touched. I wanted to be back at Cootehill with her, washing together, being friends.

I set scraps of sugared cherry into the fairy cakes. I cut green angelica to look like wings. I breathed the lovely smell of baking. Lucy, why can't you be my friend? Tin is part of me, can't you understand that? He's all I have with me from home. Even when I forget about him I need him. He could never be yours because he's mine.

The refectory table was transformed now, looking like a church altar with white linen and gold. The best white tea set had gold edgings, the crested spoons were prettily wrought. In the centre of the table was a candelabrum to be lit when the guests arrived. The log baskets were filled to bursting. Most impressive of all was the green. All down the stairway holly and ivy had been tied to the banisters and threaded with red ribbon bows. I thought of Maggie's church again. It was exciting. Cold green leaves, candlelight and sweet smells. I must change my dress next, Grandma told me, it was almost time for her guests.

I stared at myself in the long mirror. I wished I had something pink to wear. The people had different ways and ideas in Ireland. They worried more about what religion you had than what you thought about. Only Maggie had really worried about me. Are you worrying now, Maggie?

The big porch bell rang, the guests were arriving, the yearly treat had begun. The van man was first, and his daughter. She clung to him because she couldn't speak.

She had the young old face of a dwarf or a lady giant, you couldn't guess her age. Her mouth trembled, she hated strangers; she ignored my outstretched hand. Her father was proud of her, proud of her dependency, she was his speechless only child. He boasted that she was afraid of her own shadow, wouldn't let him out of her sight, she relied on him. But he relied on her help on his work rounds, putting the change into his customers' hands. Sometimes she carried shampoos and potatoes to back doors for him. She was a great girl, so she was; he was proud enough to beat the band.

The vet was next, wearing a great coat that smelled of ether. His breath smelled of drink and smoke. Grandma didn't allow smokers to smoke inside the manor house, there were no ashtrays or lighters or spills. But now she smiled gaily, he was an exception, for didn't he heal sick animals and birds? She had the place looking gorgeous as usual, he said loudly, without taking his pipe from his teeth. Gorgeous, Marm, gorgeous, and greetings to one and all here. He inspected the holly and red ribbons. Not many berries, a sign of more snow. Gorgeous, though, no other word for it. He looked at Lucy's father. All set for the punch-making? It seemed that they made it together, it was the custom. He handed a parcel to Grandma and I guessed rightly that it was drink. Mick on the mail train, Maggie's Da and that butcher, all smokey-smelling, all fond of strong drink. It made them silly and watery-eyed but made them friendly. The vet patted me on the head. This drink was special, he'd made it, a treat for Grandma to enjoy every year. The van man fingered his pioneer badge. He mustn't criticize, the vet did good work, a grand man.

The big hall was ready, the baking completed, the games were planned, when would we eat? The Cootehill sisters were a long time taking their coats off and settling their wispy hair. They wore dresses that they'd made them-selves from stockinet oddments with lace modesty vests at the neck. They both wore brooches in the shape of swans, flying. They twittered with joy over the leaves tied with red ribbon, they yearned over the white and gold plates. 'Beautiful. Beau-ootiful as always,' they chorused, slight envy behind their eyes. When it came to style they could spot it, it was their livelihood. Everything here was the height of style. Their gift was a tin painted with shamrocks, designed to hold packets of tea. 'The cup that cheers but does not inebriate,' the vet uttered portentously. At last the teapot was brought in. I had helped to polish it with pink powder and a chamois leather earlier, after arranging the scones and cakes. Lucy sat at one end with her father. I helped Grandma to pour the tea, pouring milk into the white and gold teacups. I offered the scones that I'd helped to knead.

'Gorgeous, gorgeous,' the vet murmured, topping his cup with a small flask, refusing the food.

'Beau-ootiful,' the sisters whispered, moving their mouths, peckingly like birds. The van man and his daughter both ate heartily, making a lot of crumbs on the floor and round their plates.

The first game was always Hunt the Thimble, the same games were played every year. There was Spin the Trencher, then Blind Man's Buff, all of them strange to me; I'd never played any games. Maggie had tried 'I Spy' with me, but not knowing spelling made it dull and we both liked talking the best, or looking at her film star books. Maggie had been a true friend, except when those men were about. I wouldn't think about what would happen next to me. Not knowing, not even wondering was best. The van man's daughter behaved rudely with her fairy cake. The handicapped or young babies could behave as they wished.

'Let Ula have first turn hiding the thimble. She's never played before.' Lucy's voice sounded sugar-sweet. For the sake of the van man's daughter, to humour her, the thimble was hidden in the same place always. Everyone pretended to close their eyes. 'On the frame of Grandfather's portrait,' Grandma whispered. The van man's daughter grunted with fun. It was she that found it each time. No one behaved as you'd expect in this country, especially inside their homes. 'Great girl, great girl,' her father applauded. It was Spin the Trencher next. The one who spun the board called the name of the one who must catch it. If it dropped before they got it they paid a forfeit.

'Let Ula have first turn.'

Are you trying to discomfort me, Lucy? I don't know the people's names. Grandma said she was too tired to play now, she would save her energy for the other games. Her cheeks had two flushed spots of red in them; she sat by the fire alone.

'Lucy,' I shouted, turning the trencher, dropping it. It rolled under the refectory table, falling flat before she could get it.

'I'll pay you out for that, you'll see,' she whispered.

Charades came next. 'What is Charades, Grandma, I've forgotten?'

'Poor Ula, she doesn't know.'

I was to pick one side, Lucy the other. I'd learn the rules as we played. 'I'll pick my own father,' Lucy said proudly. I called Grandma's name. Lucy had everything, she was cherished, encircled with love and care. She knew the games, knew the people, knew the mansion. And where had Grandma got to now?

'I'm here, I haven't deserted you. Just putting the bottle away.'

She and the vet emerged from the back scullery, her cheeks looked a little more red. He said, swaying slightly, that Charades was a gorgeous game, gorgeous, nothing like a game of pretend.

Like Hunt the Thimble they never changed it, they chose the same word to act every year. The interest and charm of playing was in the acting, the word they chose was 'legend'. The first scene must include the word 'leg', the second, 'end', the whole word must be said in the last one. All the games were made easy for the van man's daughter. Perhaps one day she would understand. I picked the two sisters as well as Grandma who explained what we had to act. Someone must fall and break a leg first. As we were planning the scene the van man's daughter made a terrible gobbling sound, she left her seat, rushing at us, whirling and waving her arms.

'God love her, she's excited,' apologized her father, leading her away with him. Didn't that prove now that she had a heart? She couldn't endure to watch people hurting themselves.

'I have it,' the vet said in a throaty voice. 'The word is "legend", no need to act out the play.'

Everyone clapped and applauded; the van man's daughter clapped loudest of all. Grandma said we'd go straight on now to Hide and Seek, no more Charades tonight. She didn't want any of the guests overtaxed or fatigued; she would hide first as usual, in a nice little easy place. She'd just pop out with the vet to the scullery and see that the punch-making was under way. Hot punch was a grand drink to end the evening. Lucy remarked cheekily that some people liked it at the start. Her father was to stay at the base to help the vet with the drink-making, the rest of us were to hunt in pairs.

The Cootehill sisters had each other, the daughter clung to the van man. Lucy's father and the vet would join in later, so Lucy and I were left.

'Can't I ever get away from you?' she said. 'We've been together all day.'

Each of the hunters was provided with a flashlight; the game was to be played in the dark.

'Close your eyes now everyone,' Grandma said in a thick voice, emerging from the scullery again.

The lights were switched off, we waited round the fireside. The Cootehill sisters settled their skirts. Was that the tap of strap shoes going up the stairway? Was that the grey shawl catching at the leaves?

'Grandma is going upstairs, Lucy. I'm sure I heard her.'

'She'll hide outside, she always does.'

'Outside? But the snow. And the woods, they're danger-ous.'

'Not to me they aren't. I know them.'

'But they're out of bounds. Grandma said.'

'You know nothing about it. Milksop. You know nothing about the rules.'

She laughed excitedly, this was their tradition. We must put our macs on again now. Come along, follow her. More snow had fallen since this morning when we'd dragged the leaves across the lawns; there was no trace of that now, only pure snow and some footprints. Lucy was the first out, moving quickly, picking her booted way in the light of the moon. We had no need of our torches yet, it was brilliant. I looked back at the manor house gable, shaped like a giant Christmas tree, with the moon and stars for lights. Our boots made slushing sounds. Lucy moved so quickly. I would have liked to hold her hand. She wanted to be the first to find Grandma, she didn't want me along too. She called over her shoulder to pick up my wellingtons. I was slow as well as afraid. She and Grandma knew every inch of the estate, just follow and hurry, do.

'She wouldn't be inside the old wood surely, Lucy? Not after what she said.'

We were by the holly trees where we'd cut branches. Lucy gasped. Look. Tracks. Over there. I lit the torch. Grandma must have crossed the lawns and gone straight inside the old wood.

'The snow is deeper now, Lucy. You're going too fast again.'

'Complaining again, scullery maid. I've *got* to find her first.'

Her voice was as cruel and impatient as it had been this morning. Being outside made her worse. Whatever happened, I must keep Tin, she wasn't fit for him. I wanted to get the game over and go inside. I looked back at the other seekers; their torches made dots of light.

'Lucy, the Cootehill sisters are old. The van man's daughter can't move fast. Lucy, wait for the rest.'

'Feck the lot of them,' I thought she answered, but I couldn't be sure in this snow. I could see her torch far in front of me, darting beneath the dark trees. The wellingtons were still uncomfortable, my feet slipped. The mac was too big. It seemed that the hunters lacked spirit, all nervous, all lost, all cold. Lucy should wait for us, she was selfish. Lucy, your heart is cold.

I tried to hurry, my torchlight was dimmer. Worst of all was the soft deep snow. Lucy surely wouldn't want Tin after this evening. My worst punishment was happening now. The wood felt evil and dangerous, only safe for animals and birds. Perhaps the trees will put a curse on us, or the owls peck and the swans lunge. A stag can attack and kill you, a savage fox can bite. Grandma can't have intended disturbance in her sanctuary. How much of that drink had she drunk? The snowdrifts are deep and icy, the trees are thick, where are the stars?

'Lucy, wave your torch again. Please, Lucy.'

There was a sound. Was that her chuckly voice? Was she whispering? 'This way, milksop. Over here.'

There were no lights. I pushed forward. Was that a thicket?

'Call again, Lucy. Don't leave me, please. You must stay close, it's the rule.'

Stick to your partner, whistle if you get separated, wave and flash your torch. Last one to find the quarry paid a forfeit. Was that a whistle? Was it Lucy? Was she whistling that strange little tune? She wanted Tin because I did. Being cruel gave you power.

116

I felt something like a hole. Was it a footprint? Was she trailing a wild beast? Grandma can't be in the old wood, she loves animals. I want Lucy to be my friend. Please, Lucy, I need a soul sister. Wave your torch. Be my companion. I hate you, Lucy, whistle your tune.

I heard twigs snapping, snow shifting and falling. I sensed that someone was near. I went forward, I must not be frightened. I can see something shining ahead. A glittering patch all bright and frightening, cold-looking, the shape of a twisted heart. Lucy, I can't see you. Have you found Grandma? Make a whistle. I'm by the lake.

The ground is muddy, marshy, squelchy. The marshy part at the tip of the lake. I feel something spikey. Rushes. These cold spikes are rushes in my hand. Something else, something is pulling me, someone is pulling my hand.

Lucy's hands are cool, thin-boned, delicate. Don't pull me, Lucy, I'm falling. Someone is breathing. Quick breathing, then a watery sort of gasp. There you are, Lucy, all the time.

They said afterwards that the little knife that she'd lent me that morning had been pointing downwards as I fell. Still in my pocket, the point went straight into her. She pulled, I slipped, I fell onto her, the knife pierced her white childish throat. Lucy, I can't find you. Why did you leave me? Your face is wet, why did you run? Speak, Lucy, can't you say something? Lucy, why did you run away?

Everywhere was confusion and shouting. There was moaning in my ears. The Cootehill sisters made noises of dementia. The van man told them to whisht. He would go back for the two other men, they'd bring bandages, they'd know what to do. His daughter started her noises again, sounding terrible in the dark by the lake. She clung to him, she pulled and impeded him and Lucy made no sound on the ground.

By the time help came the sisters were praying. The

combined flashlights of the hunters made a weak light in the mud. Lucy's father and the vet brought lanterns, shining them on Grandma and Lucy. Lucy hadn't spoken, nor had Grandma, who was paralysed, stiff from shock. The three of us were muddied and wet-looking, we were stained with splashes of dark. Blood looks black in the darkness. The father picked up Lucy, her hair trailed over his arm. Her hands dangled. Lucy, speak to me, I know you're teasing. Why did you run away?

The party left the old wood and walked over the lawns again. The vet led the way with the lantern, then came Lucy in her father's arms. I kept saying her name aloud over and over. If I called loudly enough she'd be all right. Lucy? I know you're teasing. Lucy? Inside the porch he turned.

'Why are you calling her? What have you done to her? Don't you realize Lucy is dead?'

ELEVEN

Grandma didn't speak until she got inside. She had been the last in the cortege through the wood. The Cootehill sisters had pulled at her hands. She was an abject sight compared with her earlier self. Inside the manor she revived a little. She told me to go upstairs and wait there until the doctor and the priest had been and gone.

'I don't want to go up. I want to stay here.'

They had put Lucy on the refectory table. They were all round her. I couldn't see.

The elder sister pushed me to the bottom of the staircase. Lucy's soul had gone to God. The doctor would come to put the seal of officialdom on her leaving. The priest would pray for her safe arrival, though of that there was not a doubt. Lucy's soul had been pure and stainless from her Christmas confession and communion, her soul would go straight to God. More lies and rubbish, I thought darkly, as I went again up the stairs. They could sign documents and pray as much as they liked. I could go into Lucy's room now if I wanted. You pulled me down, Lucy, it's your fault. Tin is mine now, for ever and ever. You shouldn't have run away.

I can hear the bell ringing for the praying and signing.

Blood looks nearly black in the dark. The grandfather in the picture will look down on them with painted eyes. All the rest will have eyes full of tears. They will bow their heads, they will cross themselves, their mouths will murmur in prayer. I never learned prayers, none of us did. Would Lucy meet Bruno now? I imagined she would despise and bully him if she could manage it. Poor Bruno, I rarely thought of him now.

When Grandma came upstairs I didn't want to look at her, I didn't want to see her candle-white face. The whites of her eyes were pink and terrible. She still managed to look severe. She leaned from her height to kiss me, just brushing her lips on my head. Maggie's kisses had been loud and smeary, often having an onion smell. Grandma's were a breath of lavender. Lucy was ready now. I could come down. I was not to indulge in self-blame for the accident. I must come and honour her remains. Thanks to the good Cootehill sisters Lucy looked radiant as a picture. God wanted her back, his holy child.

'Yes. Where though? Is she near Limbo now?'

'What are you talking about? Limbo? Lucy made a happy death.' Lucy was with the saints and the angels. Come down and see. I'd soon understand. The good sisters had been so wonderful. I would understand when I saw.

'I don't want to see her.'

'Ula.' Her voice was sharp. I must learn to do as she bid me. She would never believe that Lucy had deceived her, that she'd been a fraud, had given up praying, had not been to mass. She didn't believe in God any more. If there was a God he'd probably not want her, he would be disgusted to have her near. I didn't want to look at her, she'd been my enemy. But I must do as I was bid.

I was still wearing my cream Viyella. There was a line of mud now, along the hem. I had changed into my bedroom slippers with the brown pompoms. Grandma took my hand on the stairs.

The red bows in the greenery were gone now. There was a hushed and churchy smell. You knew I didn't like knives, Lucy. I never meant to hurt you. I hate that old wood with the lake. It's sad, it's frightening, it's dark. It's bad luck too, shaped like a twisted heart. It's your fault for going in there. The vet must have made Grandma drunk.

'There. Doesn't she look seraphic?'

I didn't think she did. She looked awful, lying there. The refectory table had been pulled well back from the fireplace. She was at the far end, in a white lace robe that reached below her feet. She looked taller now and her face was stiff as the frills on the pillow she lay on. There were lit candles at each end. Was it Grandma's nightdress she was wearing? Why couldn't they have left her in her pink? Was it muddied and bloodied after the accident? White didn't suit her, nor did frills. She looked like a tall ugly doll now, lying just where she'd sat at tea. She'd been buttering scones with those fingers; now they held rosary beads. Her face looked so stiff.

'Isn't she beau-ootiful,' they whispered. They had done this to her.

'A seraphic picture,' Grandma said.

'I don't think so at all. Why didn't you leave her pink frock on?'

Grandma's hard fingers pinched me. Bold and truculent child. The sisters both hissed with disapproval, and they after working so hard. They'd made a beautiful corpse out of Lucy. Trust the English child to complain. I had neither respect nor understanding of life here, they didn't wish to be told what to do. In any case, her pink dress had been ruined, the . . . occurrence had rendered it fit only for scraps. Lucy was so pure and holy the pink might even end as relics in the future. The white was perfect; they as dressmakers should know. They'd a deal of experience with deceased persons, they were in demand in the country around. They were sent for when loved ones

121

passed over, their piety and taste were famed. They'd been sad not to have had more flowers for her laying out, it was the wrong season of the year. There was enough holly about to fill a cathedral, but holly wasn't right for a corpse. The collar of her nightdress was turned upwards, her little red wound didn't show. I wanted to wrench her eyes open, explain, make her listen. All of this had served her right. She shouldn't have taken her knives here. I hated knives. Now I'd keep Tin.

I looked at her father standing behind us, his face set. He looked older, grey. He wasn't looking at Lucy but at the floor in front of him. He wasn't holding any beads. The candles made guttering noises, the beads in the sisters' hands clicked. Your father knows about you, Lucy, and I know. You're a fraud, you're not holy at all.

'Kneel, Ula. Try and say a prayer.'

'Why is the fire out, Grandma?'

You had to have cool air near a corpse, it seemed. I put my hands over my face again. 'Hail nonsense. Hello rubbish. You may look like a seraph to some people. I think you look like a dead doll. It's all your fault, you know it is. Oh Lucy, I wish you were here.'

Her hair was arranged glossily under the candlelight. She liked her hair pulled back from her face. A chef mustn't have hair falling about. 'I've seen you, Lucy, put your tongue to your nose.' 'Pray for us sinners now and at the hour of our death,' intoned the sisters. Their worried breathing smelled of tea.

'I think Lucy ought to have her chef's hat on, and perhaps a recipe book in her hand.'

'That's enough, Ula. Upstairs again.'

'I want to stay down here with you, Grandma. I don't like it up there alone.'

She looked sharp again. Her eyes were still pink-tinged and terrible. I was too young to stay down, too ignorant of their ways. The grown-ups would keep a watch here until the morning. 'What age is she?' one of the sisters whispered. What an impossible child. No wonder the English grew up bad.

'But I don't like it, Grandma. Please, let me stay.'

The father raised his head and looked at me but said nothing. I felt he thought I should stay. My world too had been shattered; a child's grief was potent too.

I went up to the long gallery, my brown slippers making no sound. I opened Lucy's door and went in. It was a larger room than mine with a darker carpet. The fire was out, the shutters closed. I shivered; the coldest part of me was in my head. I opened the big wardrobe; no pink dancing dress. Lucy, where are you now? You were wearing the dress when I first saw you. You left your monkey, you didn't want it. Now you have left and I'm behind.

There was nothing lying about except her knife box, with the smallest knife not in its place. A few cookery books were on the bookshelf. She'd been old ahead of her time. Her blue nightdress edged with shamrocks was under her pillow. I could sleep in her bed if I wanted; no one would know downstairs. She had a big washbasin in a recess with a light in the mirror over it. The washbasin had a crack and the pedestal was unsteady. It was the first worn object I'd seen here. Grandma had said no bathing at night-time. I would wash here in Lucy's room. I tried the hot tap; the water ran brown at first, then clean and hot. I went to my room to fetch Tin. When I got back there was a dark stain on the carpet spreading wider and wider. I turned the tap off. What would Grandma say? Would it seep through the ceiling and splash on top of Lucy? Would it hiss on the candle flames? I tried mopping with her face flannel. Then I washed and got into her bed.

I gave a jump when the bedroom door opened, expecting Grandma's disapproving face.

'Who is in here?' the father's voice asked. Who was in his beloved daughter's bed? He'd come up to say goodnight to me. Why was I not in my own bed? I tried to sound adult and casual.

'I'm in Lucy's room tonight. I thought it would make a change.'

I pulled the sheet up, I didn't want him seeing me in her nightdress, but his own grief was his main concern. His face looked like the oldest in the world, grooved with sadness round the eyes and mouth. I would have liked to comfort him, but didn't know how to. I didn't think he'd like me on his knee or holding on to him. He stood awkwardly, hanging his hands. I looked at his broad fingertips again; the fingers themselves were quite thin. His nails, though short, had conspicuous half-moons.

'I thought . . . I thought that . . .' I expect that he'd thought I was Lucy, in her bed up here, not dead downstairs. He was bound to miss her, I told him in a wise voice. One day it would seem like a bad dream.

'You're too young to have all this to bear.'

'Yes. I didn't mean to have that knife. I hate knives.'

I didn't tell him that I liked wearing her nightdress and lying in her bed. Being there made me miss her less. I wondered if he knew about her knife-brandishing and cruelty and how much I'd envied her.

He picked up Tin from the eiderdown, his palm covering the painted spots. Lucy had never owned toys like other children, she'd stopped playing with bears and dolls. He'd encouraged her to be practical and resourceful. He would be thrown onto his own resources now, he'd be put to the test. When all this was over he must go back to the city and his livelihood. Life would never be the same. I thought of his students returning from the holiday to a house without Lucy. The salmon-pink kitchen would feel melancholy without Lucy whistling and humming while she concocted her stuffing and stews. Who would put scraps out for the birds and order her father about? The animals with the hotel names would be given away. What would happen to

124

her school uniform and her chef's aprons? Surely no one would want to use her knives?

'My father died you know. And my baby brother. He was quite young really, just a few weeks old.'

I wanted him to know that he wasn't alone with his sorrow, that I'd some deaths to bear as well. I hadn't missed my father, I didn't mind not having one until I saw Lucy with hers. He said quietly that he'd been self-indulgent, he'd tried to burden me with his own loss. I'd already suffered too much. I was so young. His excuse was that I had a listening heart. Forgive him. Could he put my clothes on the bed? He removed them from the small stuffed armless chair and pulled it near to me. This was where he used to sit with Lucy; they liked quiet talks before she slept. The Christmas party last year had been perfect, everything had gone with a swing.

'Did you play Hide and Seek outside last year?'

'Of course. The same games every year.' It was their ritual: the same decorations, hiding the thimble in the same place, acting the same word for Charades. His mother always hid first in the old wood, on the edge by the holly trees. Only . . . this time she'd gone inside. Her eyes were weak, she'd not been well recently. Their guests loved the tradition of the party, they felt bonded and needed. What would happen now?

'Don't think about it. I'll tell you about my family.'

About Bonnie and Tor, my two sisters who had no time for anyone but each other and never any time for me. How Bonnie was derived from the word 'good' in Latin, though Bonnie had never been good to me. Tor was short for Hortense, a Roman clan name. They had their governess in Shottermill, they were happy there. I had never had a true friend, that's why I wanted Lucy. Then I told him about Maggie, how I'd helped her in the kitchen on Sundays while Nurse stayed with Bruno upstairs. I'd grated salt, made crumbs from bread crusts, I'd emptied rubbish into the bins. I told him about her film star books and cutting out pictures of stars. How Maggie had danced the jig for me. Did no one dance any jigs here? I used to love being with Maggie. It all changed when Bruno died. I wanted to explain it to him. How Nurse, who wasn't a proper nurse but a great-aunt with black blood in her, had loved Bruno truly. When he died she'd gone off her head. I didn't tell about the pot flying out of the window. I wanted him to understand about my old world, about the kitchen and Maggie's comfortable smell.

'And your mother? Where does she fit in? How is she? How does she feel?'

'"Feel?" Mamma?'

I never thought about Mamma having feelings. What was Mamma really like? I told him about her wanting to become an actress. I couldn't imagine her being like the ones in Maggie's pictures, with big lollopers, big teeth and behinds. My sisters were going away to school soon. Mamma hadn't said what I would do yet. I wanted to stay being a child. Though childhood was miserable and terrible, being grown-up might be worse. Maggie had said that Mamma might sell our house and leave.

He said I shouldn't pay too much attention to what Maggie said.

'Who? Maggie? Why?'

I wanted him to be interested in me, to question me instead of thinking of Lucy. He must know she'd been a bully, she'd been far from sweet and angelic to me. I liked his neat hair with grey streaks in it. I liked him not smelling of drink. His coat and his brogues matched each other, like turf sods just frosted with snow. I wanted him to tell me where Lucy would be taken. If I knew that I might not worry about where I'd go next. I asked when I would see Maggie.

He said it was unlikely that I'd see her for a long time, if ever. I ought to forget Maggie now.

'What happened? What did she do?'

It would be ill-advised, he said, to contact her or her family again.

'She had a brother, you know. Under the Christmas tree, lying there. I wanted to tell Lucy, I didn't get a chance.'

Someone must listen now, I had to explain. The Ma's tears had sounded so desolate. All that horror, the liver and blood. Some grown-ups seemed so sad. Maggie loved me. Her Da was kind. Irish families knew how to love, she had said so. Was her family different, was it religion? She'd told me too about Ireland having no snakes or toads, as well as no king or queen.

He said mutual respect and tolerance were universal. In some families, no matter which country, things went wrong. It all started from within the family, success or failure later in life. Maggie's mother was weak in her mind. Maggie herself had been a mother, did I know that?

'Poor thing. What is it called? Where is the baby?'

Her child had been born prematurely, more than that he didn't know. He'd nothing against Maggie, she'd gone to England to get away. He'd been horrified by the poverty, the overcrowding; slum dwellers paid a price the world over. Her family were deprived.

'Yes but did you see their Christmas tree? Did you see Joe too?'

He said Joe, in his view, was jail fodder. It was the mother he felt pity for. So many mothers had it hard. I thought of my own mother again, Maggie's mother, Grandma. I wondered where Lucy's own mother was.

He sighed groaningly again, his thoughts returning to his own loss. When he leaned to hug me his eyes weren't thinking of me but of Lucy, his pride and delight. He tried to make his mouth smile as he left me. Don't go, Lucy's father, think of me, I'm here.

I put my face into her pillow again. I had her nightdress, I had her room. I had Tin.

The elder sister came in the morning, her face bleached dry from her tears. Crying and exhaustion made her more kindly to me, or perhaps it was the effect of the death. Her cheeks felt rough as her lace frilling. Her voice was even more whispery now. She fumbled her hands. Look at your clothes, childey; who tossed them like that over the bed? You couldn't learn tidiness too early, an orderly room pleased the saints. I asked her where Grandma was.

It seemed she was unwell. The night had been too much for her, her heart was never strong. She was in her bed now, while Lucy's father was seeing to things. I guessed that soon the men with the dark car would come for Lucy. She'd be leaving the manor soon for good. The sister told me to go through to the back kitchen for my breakfast. So I wouldn't have to look at the refectory table again.

The younger sister was stirring porridge. She wore Grandma's apron which reached to the floor. I asked if I could have brown sugar with it and she said why not? Extra sweetness would be no harm on this day. Grandma had strode up and down yesterday, with her porridge bowl in her hand, pausing to peer at Grandfather's picture. Today she lay in her bed sorrowing, with a weakly beating heart. I took a spoonful of porridge, having stirred the sugar to runniness. I swallowed, it wouldn't go down. I stirred again with the crested spoon. I couldn't eat it, it tasted vile. The sister said not to worry, porridge could be difficult. Would I take some toast fingers instead? And some milk in this pretty cup now. There, wasn't that quite the thing? It was cold outside, but not too cold for a walk. A little walk would do me no harm. Then, after I got back, later, things would be . . . normal again.

'I suppose you mean that Lucy's body will be gone then? Will the fires be lit again?'

She answered with a fresh gush of tears. She wiped her face on the apron string. Respect for the dead was something I'd not learned. Go out now through the back door quickly. Ah, what it was to be a child.

The wellingtons that I'd worn yesterday were by the back door waiting. She joined her sister for a last round of tears and prayers. The boots didn't feel as big and alien. The raincoat felt damp and cold. There was no blood on it. Had the sisters cleaned it? I put my hand into the pocket; there was no knife. I hadn't wanted the knife, I hated knives. All of this was Lucy's fault. I didn't want to walk in the new wood either, or anywhere outside at all. How awful she'd looked in that lace.

The back of the manor was in shadow. I breathed in the icy air. I walked through the yard past the bins and out-houses. The early sun came out, a faint warmth shone on my face. In the bottom of the right-hand pocket was a small rent; I poked my finger through. What would happen to me? Soon Lucy's father would be going back. I had killed Lucy yesterday in holy Ireland. I was the first one to walk on this snow, all brilliant and silvery white. Ahead of me stretched the new wood with the Christmas trees, little pointed green shapes, hundreds of them, all similarly sized. This was Maggie's green as a parable Ireland, under white as chastity snow. I'd expected to be loved and needed here, the country of legend and lore. I had envied Lucy, I had hated her, loved her. I was alive, she was dead. I walked between the lines of trees, making tracks where no one had trodden. Up one avenue of trees and down the next, my feet pointing outwards, crushing the silvery snow.

I heard a sound, I looked upwards. A bird was flying over the manor, a long-tailed brilliant shape. I saw the tail feath-ers trailing, I could see the small head and small cold eyes. It came to rest in front of me, I could see the turquoise blue neck feathers shining, the gold and brown eyes on the tail. It looked at me impassively, then rose slowly and flew back over the gabled roof. It had left a feather in the snow, small and fluffy with a hint of iridescent blue sheen.

'Hail. All hail. Hail,' I whispered. I ran back into the house.

'I've seen the peacock. I've seen the peacock,' I told the sisters. Where was Grandma, I must tell her.

'Aye, go you up to her. Don't make a noise mind.'

She was in her bed looking older and smaller, her face between the hanging white plaits looked thin. Her eyes looked as if she'd cried the colour from them. She put out her hand.

'I saw the peacock, the ghost peacock. It's not a ghost, it's real.'

'That's grand. For your luck, child. Grand.'

'What's wrong? Are you ill, Grandma?'

'Just resting. That's grand about the bird. They say that those it looks on will be in for a bit of a change.'

'He looked at me. He had little hard eyes, round like beads.'

I showed her the curled fluff of feather, the proof that he'd been there. From under the wing, she thought.

'Has Lucy left the manor now?'

'She has gone, yes. But you must stay. Stay as long as you'd like to.'

'You mean you'd like me to? You want me? Me?'

She whispered that Lucy had needed a friend, that she'd loved me. I must stay here, treat the manor as my home. She'd already spoken to Lucy's father. He'd make the arrangements. And my two sisters could come too. I could have anyone I wished to stay here. Anyone I wanted. Did I like the idea?

TWELVE

Bonnie and Tor came to the manor. That spring and summer I was happy, I blotted what had happened earlier from my mind. I remember the games we played, I can still hear the sounds our voices made.

We kept to the gallery at first, hardly whispering. Then we crept down the wide stairs, running round the refectory table, then gradually out on the porch. Bonnie and Tor were afraid of Grandma, but their fear turned to respect and then need. Grandma didn't vary, she was there constantly, though apart from cooking and eating meals with us she stayed in her room. Her health worsened after Lucy died.

The summer that year was long and dry. We stayed alone apart from meals. We played late into the evenings, staying on the upper lawn close to the manor's grey walls. We knew that Grandma was upstairs, we were protected. My sisters never asked about Lucy, or what had happened down by the lake. They didn't look towards the old wood or want to go there, nor did the new wood at the back interest us. We were involved in our games and ourselves on the upper lawn, nothing else mattered. I was included at last. Once in the night I thought I heard the peacock crying, but it could have been an owl. We loved the bats that flew over our heads in the twilight, we chased them and tried to copy their sound. We ran barefoot races, we played statues. They taught me Grandmother's Steps. I loved the feel and smell of the dewy grass under my thighs as I rolled head over heels, I loved to hear Bonnie and Tor call. I loved running round the upper lawn till I was giddy, dazed, touched with glory. I loved holding their hands, touched with joy. I put the past behind me that summer. I never saw Maggie again.

That September the war came and another life started. I went with my sisters to school. During the holidays we stayed there. Mamma joined a company, touring to entertain the forces, but I was never as lonely again because I had Bonnie and Tor. They were mine and I was theirs.

I never went back to Ireland. It all happened a long time ago. I came across Tin in a box of old trinkets; there was a brown scrap of feather too. Tin is smaller than I remember, and shabbier, his painted spots have gone. But for finding him I might believe that I'd imagined the events of that strange sad Christmas. I don't think I have exaggerated, but I wonder.

URSULA HOLDEN

Wider Pools

The old swimming pool has cracked tiles, cramped cubicles, insects that fall from the glass dome into the water. But Shirley prefers to swim there, to float and muse. The presence of her fat, complaining sister Zee cannot spoil its pleasures.

But Shirley knows she has work to do, a life to reassemble after drifting away from family, past sorrows, turning points. She intends to use the summer self-indulgently, to piece things together again. She begins – has her hair cut, buys new clothes, plans to write. Then events step in. Past, present and future come together in a series of crises that force Shirley into a new life and a new appreciation of who she is.

Ursula Holden's latest novel sparkles with mordant humour, observation and undertones of horror, confirming her as one of the most gifted of today's writers.

'Concentrated, complex and comic'
LONDON MAGAZINE

'Miss Holden is an inspired and original talent'
AUBERON WAUGH

'Stylish, staccato prose and [a] faultless ear for dialogue'
IRISH TIMES

'Deft and compact'
TIMES LITERARY SUPPLEMENT

URSULA HOLDEN

Eric's Choice

On the surface, Eric Caive-Propp, a teacher whose life is determined by taste and control, has little in common with Violet Stubbs – vulgar, temperamental, daughter of a market trader in garish trinkets. Yet Eric chose Violet. She had been one of his pupils – immature and selfish – and he married her.

Eric takes Violet at face value, believing he can mould his seventeen-year-old bride to suit the niceties and exquisiteness of the house on the green, decorated by his art-collector mother. But he is witness to a change that transforms his home into a 'purple paradise' of gaudy knick-knacks and tubular steel . . .

Eric and Violet's stormy relationship is the meat of Ursula Holden's hilarious and biting novel, which explores family loves and lives with an acid humour and unmistakable originality.

'Ursula Holden is a highly original writer . . . Her dialogue is hard to fault, her characters are usually convincing and she has an abrupt, disconcerting wit'
IRISH TIMES

'Ursula Holden is adept at exposing the muddy complexities of her characters, the lurking bestiality behind the human proprieties'
TIMES LITERARY SUPPLEMENT

'Eric's Choice is witty, bleak and exact'
Andrew Sinclair, THE TIMES

VIOLET TREFUSIS

Broderie Anglaise

Broderie Anglaise presents, in fictional form, the key event of Violet Trefusis' youth: her love affair with Vita Sackville-West.

Alexa, a young bluestocking novelist – 'one of those women who having no bloom to lose improve with age' – has an affair with a personable aristocrat. Previously he had been on the point of marrying his cousin, Anne. Anne's spectre haunts their affair. So does his vulgar, malicious mother in her old dressing gown and jewels. When Alexa finally meets her rival from the past – at a finely observed tea-party – everyone's role changes.

'It is a love story full of seduction and worldliness and lingering scents . . . it comes to life not because Trefusis is dealing with a real-life affair, but because she succeeds in showing how passion totters on some very flimsy pedestals.'
THE TIMES

'A fictional account of the author's affair with Vita Sackville-West, which at the time was thought to be scandalous, and a work which can also be seen as a reply to Virginia Woolf's *Orlando*. Provides further insights into the extraordinary and complex personalities of all three women.'
GUARDIAN

Methuen Modern Fiction

While every effort is made to keep prices low, it is sometimes necessary to increase prices at short notice. Methuen Paperbacks reserves the right to show new retail prices on covers which may differ from those previously advertised in the text or elsewhere.

The prices shown below were correct at the time of going to press.

☐	413 52310 1	**Silence Among the Weapons**	John Arden	£2.50
☐	413 52890 1	**Collected Short Stories**	Bertolt Brecht	£3.95
☐	413 53090 6	**Scenes From Provincial Life**	William Cooper	£2.95
☐	413 59970 1	**The Complete Stories**	Noël Coward	£4.50
☐	413 54660 8	**Londoners**	Maureen Duffy	£2.95
☐	413 41620 8	**Genesis**	Eduardo Galeano	£3.95
☐	413 42400 6	**Slow Homecoming**	Peter Handke	£3.95
☐	413 42250 X	**Mr Norris Changes Trains**	Christopher Isherwood	£3.50
☐	413 59630 3	**A Single Man**	Christopher Isherwood	£3.50
☐	413 56110 0	**Prater Violet**	Christopher Isherwood	£2.50
☐	413 41590 2	**Nothing Happens in Carmincross**	Benedict Kiely	£3.50
☐	413 58920 X	**The German Lesson**	Siegfried Lenz	£3.95
☐	413 60230 3	**Non-Combatants and Others**	Rose Macaulay	£3.95
☐	413 54210 6	**Entry Into Jerusalem**	Stanley Middleton	£2.95
☐	413 59230 8	**Linden Hills**	Gloria Naylor	£3.95
☐	413 55230 6	**The Wild Girl**	Michèle Roberts	£2.95
☐	413 57890 9	**Betsey Brown**	Ntozake Shange	£3.50
☐	413 51970 8	**Sassafrass, Cypress & Indigo**	Ntozake Shange	£2.95
☐	413 53360 3	**The Erl-King**	Michel Tournier	£4.50
☐	413 57600 0	**Gemini**	Michel Tournier	£4.50
☐	413 14710 X	**The Women's Decameron**	Julia Voznesenskaya	£3.95
☐	413 59720 2	**Revolutionary Road**	Richard Yates	£4.50

All these books are available at your bookshop or newsagent, or can be ordered direct from the publisher. Just tick the titles you want and fill in the form below.

Methuen Paperbacks, Cash Sales Department, PO Box 11, Falmouth, Cornwall TR10 109EN.

Please send cheque or postal order, no currency, for purchase price quoted and allow the following for postage and packing:

UK   60p for the first book, 25p for the second book and 15p for each additional book ordered to a maximum charge of £1.90.

BFPO and Eire   60p for the first book, 25p for the second book and 15p for each next seven books, thereafter 9p per book.

Overseas   £1.25 for the first book, 75p for the second book and 28p for each subsequent
Customers   title ordered.

NAME (Block Letters) ....

ADDRESS ....

....